"I don't want you to ask me to be your wife because you think you owe it to me—out of some kind of obligation."

"If you think that, then you really do not know me."

With her hat removed, the breeze blew Delphine's hair across her face and she reached up and absently drew it back, combing her fingers through it and sweeping it behind her ears, unconscious of how seductive the gesture was to Laurence. He stood absolutely still, watching her with a look that was possessive. As she looked at him, something in his expression made Delphine flush and catch her breath, and she dropped her arm self-consciously. The moment was intimate, warm and vibrantly alive. His vitality at such close quarters alarmed her, but she did not move away.

"No," she uttered quietly as she held his gaze with her own. "I don't know you, Laurence—not really."

"We can soon remedy that." Taking her hand, he drew her close. Lowering his head, he skimmed his lips over hers. "Delphine, I would like to kiss you."

Author Note

Conveniently Wed to a Spy is set in 1793. I have always been fascinated by the French Revolution. It was a turbulent time in France's history that saw the execution of King Louis XVI and Queen Marie Antoinette, which gave rise to the Republic and, later, Napoleon Bonaparte.

I wanted to write a story that touched on the Revolution while concentrating on the conflict between my two main characters.

Love is a world away from Delphine's life when she is given an assignment to assist in the escape of an English spy from the infamous Conciergerie prison in Paris. It's a rocky road they travel as they make their way out of France—but then, the road to true love is never easy.

HELEN DICKSON

Conveniently
Wed to a Spy

HARLEQUIN®
HISTORICAL™

ISBN-13: 978-1-335-40777-1

Conveniently Wed to a Spy

Copyright © 2022 by Helen Dickson

For questions and comments about the quality of this book,
please contact us at CustomerService@Harlequin.com.

Harlequin Enterprises ULC
22 Adelaide St. West, 41st Floor
Toronto, Ontario M5H 4E3, Canada
www.Harlequin.com

Printed in U.S.A.

Helen Dickson was born and still lives in South Yorkshire, UK, with her retired farm manager husband. Having moved out of the busy farmhouse where she raised their two sons, she now has more time to indulge in her favorite pastimes. She enjoys being outdoors, traveling, reading and music. An incurable romantic, she writes for pleasure. It was a love of history that drove her to writing historical fiction.

Books by Helen Dickson

Harlequin Historical

The Devil Claims a Wife
The Master of Stonegrave Hall
Mishap Marriage
A Traitor's Touch
Caught in Scandal's Storm
Lucy Lane and the Lieutenant
Lord Lansbury's Christmas Wedding
Royalist on the Run
The Foundling Bride
Carrying the Gentleman's Secret
A Vow for an Heiress
The Governess's Scandalous Marriage
Reunited at the King's Court
Wedded for His Secret Child
Resisting Her Enemy Lord
A Viscount to Save Her Reputation
Enthralled by Her Enemy's Kiss
To Catch a Runaway Bride
Conveniently Wed to a Spy

Castonbury Park

The Housemaid's Scandalous Secret

Visit the Author Profile page
at Harlequin.com for more titles.

Chapter One

Paris—1793

Moving swiftly through the darkness, the wagon carrying Delphine and Jacques, her accomplice, made its way along the narrow, winding alleyways of Paris towards the Conciergerie on the riverside. The surrounding streets were relatively empty just now, but come tomorrow the tumbrils would roll along these same streets carrying their terror-filled passengers to their deaths in the Place de la Révolution.

Dark clouds had been gathering all day. There had been a stillness in the air for the past hour—the calm before the storm. It was the kind of eerie stillness, of quietness, that made one imagine that anything could happen. There was a rumbling in the distance and forked lightning shot across the sky. Several drops of rain fell. Delphine pulled her hood further over her head as the clouds burst. By the time they crossed the river the rain was hitting the ground with such force it bounced up again, which could prove to be a blessing by keeping the citizens of Paris indoors.

Since her arrival in Paris, the stress of the situation pressed down upon Delphine. It was not the place to be in this brutal time of upheaval and turmoil, brought about by the people who were living with intolerable taxes and starvation. Since the Bastille had been pulled down by the mob in eighty-nine, it was as if France was caught in the jaws of a relentless and terrible machine which seemed impossible to stop. The things she had seen in the city since the revolution had begun had brought her to the conclusion that the overthrow of the established order was not a thing to be undertaken lightly.

She recognised that she had precious little time for working out strategies and that she must keep her wits about her. In theory what she had to do was so simple—to collect an English spy from the Conciergerie, take him to the safe house and leave for the coastal town of Granville to the west the following day. This would be easy to accomplish were it not for the National Guard patrolling the streets on the lookout for suspicious-looking citizens and those on the well-guarded gates leading out of the city through which commoners and taxable goods must pass.

Halting close to the prison walls, without a word, for they both knew what they had to do, Delphine climbed down from the cart and made her way to the entrance, confident in the knowledge that should things go awry Jacques, forever watchful, would spring to her aid. Her rain-soaked cloak hung in heavy woollen folds. She breathed in the damp air. How she had dreaded coming here.

This task wasn't like the others, when she had secreted families out of France to escape the terror. This time she had been given the task of having a man smuggled out of the Conciergerie, the most infamous prison in Paris, where anyone who was considered an enemy of the Republic was incarcerated. In these days of terror, the Conciergerie was filled with aristocrats awaiting trial. Her superior, Sir Godfrey Bucklow, had told her the prisoner was well connected and popular at the English court and an intelligence agent. Apart from that she knew nothing about him—nor did she wish to. It was better that way. The less they knew about each other the better.

With a shudder and bent on her purpose, she entered the grim building, the occasional lantern lighting her way. A guard with a bushy black beard and wearing a red cap and the tricolour was slumped in a corner. On seeing Delphine he got up. He was a man who outwardly lived and breathed the revolution, but was not averse to taking a purse of gold coins in exchange for a prisoner. Everything would be in place to move the prisoner—the network controlled from London would have seen to that.

'Who goes there?'

'Are you Gaspard Ducat?'

'I am.'

'You are expecting me,' she said in a low voice, speaking perfect French. 'I have come for the Englishman.'

Without a word, after glancing around to make sure they were alone, the guard nodded her forward. The stench coming from inside the Conciergerie was indescribable and Delphine almost retched. With knowledge of the full horror of this place her heartbeat quickened.

'Wait here. You have payment?'

'Yes—when I see the Englishman.'

He looked at her hard. Satisfied that she was the person he had been told to expect, he turned and disappeared into the gloom.

Delphine kept to the shadows. How the guard would explain the disappearance of the Englishman wasn't her concern, but she had no doubt that before morning his disappearance would have been noted and a hue and cry would ensue. She had half accomplished her part of the task. It was carrying out the rest of it that worried her. They had to get to the safe house. Fortunately it wasn't far.

After what seemed to Delphine an eternity, the guard returned, a man following close behind. He was not as wretched as Delphine had expected. He was tall, his clothes having seen better days, and through a rent in his shirt beneath his green frock coat his lean, muscled body showed. Above his dark tan boots, his skin-tight breeches were pale grey. His dark hair had not been combed and hung loose about his shoulders.

What struck her immediately was that there was nothing weak about this man. Even in this miserable state he was quite magnificent. Robbed of the trappings of the gentry, the man showed through. As she held his gaze she marvelled at what fascinating eyes he had. They were a brilliant green, or were they the turquoise blue of the Cornish sea in summertime? They stared out of a face pale from long incarceration. They focused on her.

'God's teeth!' he breathed. 'A woman.'

'As you see,' Delphine replied in clipped tones.

Her clear voice had an imperious ring that made the Englishman's eyebrows arch. His mouth broke out into a lopsided grin. His thick lashes and black brows framed dancing eyes, defiant, despite his long imprisonment which, to anyone else, would have humbled them. An inch-long scar dragged his right eyelid slightly down, giving him an expression of irony. He made a bow.

'Good evening to you, little lady.'

Taken by surprise by his ill-timed gallantry, her eyes widened. 'Good evening,' she replied coolly, in no mood to engage in polite banter.

Gaspard Ducat shook his head, making a tsking sound. 'A woman trying to smuggle prisoners out of Paris! Will wonders never cease?'

The Englishman grinned at Delphine, a flicker of amused respect glinting in his eyes. 'A wonder indeed. I thought the very same thing. Have we met?'

'No, we have not,' she assured him, irritated by what appeared to be his inability to grasp the seriousness of the situation and his seeming lack of urgency.

'No, I am certain of it now, for having once made your acquaintance that would be something I should never forget. But that you should do this for a stranger is gratifying and quite remarkable. Are you French?'

'Half-French. I trust you will not hold that against me. Now please hurry. This is not a tea party. There's no time to be lost, so keep quiet,' she ordered sharply, having no wish to indulge further in this conversation with this Englishman. The order shot out, but the smile did not fade from that fascinating face.

'I am yours to command,' he said, making the mockery of a bow.

He had a deep voice, warm and encompassing. There was laughter in it and at any other time it would make her laugh, too, but this was not the time.

Producing a purse heavy with gold coin from beneath her cloak, Delphine handed it to the guard. Opening it, he peered inside, removing one of the coins. It gleamed in the fitful light of the lantern and raised a satisfied smile on his lips.

'The guard will be changing shortly,' he growled. 'You will be missed and they will come after you so go, be away with you.'

'Come along,' Delphine said to the Englishman. 'We have to leave here.' She was conscious of him walking close behind her, his tall frame coiling and snapping with energy. Reaching the cart, she lifted a cloak from the back. 'Here, cover yourself and get in the back. I wouldn't like you to catch a chill after we've gone to all this trouble to get you out of the Conciergerie.' She looked at him, thinking his eyes danced for a moment, but the elusive lopsided grin did not reappear.

Throwing the cloak around his shoulders, he hoisted his lean, rangy body up into the back of the cart with an agility Delphine could only wonder at, making himself comfortable on the hay-covered boards. With a need for haste, she climbed up beside Jacques and they left the Conciergerie. Back through the streets they went, eventually disappearing into the network of alleyways in the poor quarter of Paris. A particular stench arose from the gutters to assail her nostrils and touch like icy fingers upon her deepest fears. It was the stench of poverty, the foul, unacceptable smell of humanity at its lowest.

Delphine prayed they would not attract the attention of the National Guard or a suspicious citizen on the lookout for anyone who opposed the Republic. The rain continued to fall, the horse plodding instinctively over the greasy cobbles, slippery with mud and refuse. Turning her head, she looked at the Englishman lying on his back, his face upturned to the rain, as though he welcomed the feel of the cold wetness on his skin. A bolt of lightning flashed, lighting up his features. He was handsome, she thought, his face lean and angular because of the lack of proper nourishment.

She stared at him, utterly taken aback by his open, easy manner when they were in the utmost danger— and worse, by her instant awareness of the powerful masculinity that radiated from him despite his sorry state. She recognised authority when she saw it. Everything about this illustrious Englishman bespoke power, control and command. His devil-may-care attitude had immediately set her teeth on edge. They were to be together for several days and there was no escaping the fact that he posed a threat to her equilibrium. Despite knowing nothing whatsoever about him, she was already beginning to dismiss him as an arrogant member of the English nobility, possibly a rake, who was used to kicking his heels in some of London's most fashionable houses before seeking an exciting diversion from his humdrum life and deciding to play the spy.

From the back of the wagon Lord Laurence Alexander Beaumont, Fourth Baron Beaumont, opened his eyes and looked up into the dark sky. The feeling of freedom was overwhelming. Emotions were churning within his chest, but he couldn't relax, not until he was out of Paris for good. Being incarcerated for so long and the feeling of impotence that went with it had, at times, become overwhelming if he started to fantasise about getting out.

He pulled himself up to take stock of his whereabouts. His features were quiet and intent. A sense of purpose and hope filled his heart and mind and was etched in every line of his body. An aura of authority and power seemed to surround him and he possessed a haughty reserve that, despite his earlier easy manner, now set him apart from his young saviour. There was something about his eyes, shadowed with some deep-felt emotion and a mocking cynicism, as though he found the whole world a dubious place to be.

As an agent of the English government, having been caught out in a plot to save King Louis XVI of France, who had gone to the guillotine in January of that year, he had been arrested and condemned by the tribunal. Fully comprehending that nothing could possibly save him from the guillotine but a miracle, he had remained incarcerated inside the Conciergerie to await the day of his execution, where torture and deprivation had almost driven him to the brink of madness.

He had struggled to retain his grip on sanity, sustaining himself by focusing his mind on escaping his tormentors and returning to his own fireside. Throughout the long months of imprisonment, in all his turbulent thoughts, in all the heated workings of his heart and mind, he had stood against resignation and mercifully his hold on life had remained strong. He was impatient to plant his feet on England's soil once more.

The tavern where they were to spend the night was tucked away in a rundown area of Paris that was rife with all manner of low life roaming the streets and back alleyways that were dark and evil smelling. An iron lamp above the door cast a dim patch of light on to the greasy cobblestones below. Getting down, Jacques took the horse's bridle.

'I'll spend the night in the stable with the horse. I'll be away first thing.'

A man in his forties and a native of Guernsey, Jacques, who lived with his wife in St Peter Port, was the owner of a fishing boat. The plight of those trying to flee France's tyranny had touched his heart. It was on this basis that he had offered his services to Sir Godfrey Bucklow, who was a native of Cornwall and worked for the British Intelligence Service. Jacques was a man of few words and during the two years Delphine had worked with him, a peculiar kind of friendship had developed between them. He had family in Paris and was concerned for their safety. It was already arranged that they would part company and she would complete the assignment without him.

'Thank you, Jacques. I'll see you before you go. I intend to make an early start with the Englishman. The gates out of Paris will be thronging with people. I'll see you have some supper sent out.'

'Good Lord!' muttered the Englishman, casting a wary eye over the inn's unappealing façade. 'What is this place?'

'Safe—at least I pray that is so tonight. It is not frequented by respectable clientele. A den of thieves is how I would describe it—although since we have nothing of substance to attract them then we should be left alone.'

Shoving open the door to the tavern, Delphine cast a sharp eye round the murky interior. It was a single public room, small and low ceilinged, the walls yellowed with tobacco smoke. Close to a soot-blackened hearth a couple of dubious characters sat huddled at a table, smoking pipes. They eyed the newcomers with suspicion before resuming their conversation. The Englishman's initial show of gallantry had disappeared as he looked around with a wary, brooding gaze, filling the tavern with his presence. The landlord gave them a hard stare before nodding a half-familiar gesture to Delphine.

'Two brandies, Maurice—make them large ones. Take one to Jacques and something to eat if you would be so kind.'

'I will stick to beer,' the Englishman said. When she shot him a curious glance he smiled thinly. 'Not having tasted the stuff for nigh on twelve months, until I am safely aboard a vessel heading for England, I will keep a clear head.'

She nodded. 'As you wish. Make that wine for me, Maurice.'

'You are familiar with this place, that much is obvious,' the Englishman murmured, taking in his surroundings.

She looked at him with cold eyes that gave nothing away. 'Yes. Maurice is to be trusted—for a price. Like the guard at the Conciergerie, his loyalty is easily bought for a full purse. We have an understanding. He won't betray us.'

'Where is your accomplice?'

'Bedded down with the horse,' she answered, sitting at a table in an alcove. 'He's also on the lookout for unwelcome visitors. It's not often the tavern is bothered by the guard, but we must be ready to move in case that should happen.'

The Englishman joined her, sitting across from her at the stained table and stretching his long legs out in front of him. A deep groove etched itself into his brow and his mouth curved slightly in a one-sided smile that did not reach his eyes. That bright green gaze seemed to see right through her defences and that small scar that dragged on his right eyelid added an illusion of savagery barely held in check.

She sensed his continued amazement along with an underlying resentment that he should owe his freedom to a woman. Clearly this wasn't what he'd expected. His expression became suddenly thoughtful and he inspected her face as if something puzzled him.

'Do you always subject people to such close scrutiny when you meet them for the first time?' Delphine asked directly, irritated by it. 'I am not used to being looked at like that and find it extremely disagreeable. Is there something wrong with my face that makes you examine it so thoroughly?'

He laughed softly. 'Forgive my boldness, but when I look at you I think unaccountably of imps and elves and things, and have half a mind to demand whether you have bewitched the guards at the Conciergerie, casting a spell on them in order to procure my release.'

'I will not argue the point, but I assure you, sir, since you know that British agents here in Paris have plotted to secure your release, it is not my intention to disrupt the workings of the Conciergerie. Quite the opposite, in fact.'

With a look that betrayed mild surprise, he nodded. 'I'm still not convinced.' His gaze continued to rest lightly on her face.

They sat in silence, Delphine with her wine and the Englishman with his ale, relishing the drink after so long an abstinence. Delphine took a long drink of her wine, so long that he laughed as she placed the glass on the table.

'What a beautiful drunkard you are.'

A stinging retort sprang to Delphine's lips, but she swallowed it. 'The past few hours have been fraught. Liquor—not that I am in the habit of imbibing too much—will settle my nerves.'

'Are you not afraid to be in the company of a prisoner of the Conciergerie? Does it not scare you?'

'No. Should I be?'

He shook his head as the fire crackled and hissed as the landlord stirred its heart back to life before disappearing to the back. 'You are quite safe with me. You are helping me. Why would I hurt you?'

She shrugged. 'I don't know you. You are just one of Mr Pitt's agents. They are active all over France. That is all I need to know. All I want to know. It is best that way. You will know me as Sophie and you are travelling as my husband under the name of Claude Blanchard until we part company. Is that understood?'

He nodded. 'I am grateful to you.'

'There is no need for gratitude. I have my own reasons for being in Paris. I am looking for something.'

'For someone, I suspect.'

'Yes, someone who has become lost in this madness that grips France just now.'

A boy appeared from the kitchen at the back of the room with some unappetising-looking food, which they ate in silence. The two men got up and left.

'What was it like—inside the Conciergerie?' she asked when the boy had left.

'There are so many prisoners. Those who have been tried are held together in a huge common cell,

waiting to be taken to the guillotine. The revolutionaries should be proud of themselves, for there, at
least, they have succeeded in levelling the classes.
The more money one has to pay the guards for luxu-
ries the better the accommodation—even though they
may be fodder for the blade the next day.'

'What good is wealth and luxury in the face of
such a dreadful fate—to be rounded up like cattle
for the slaughter? I know. I have seen the worst of it,'
she uttered quietly, trying not to think of the shadowy
figures that paraded across her mind just now. 'Were
you subjected to interrogation?'

He nodded. 'In the beginning, before being
dumped in an underground hellhole, but I gave no
account. I was kept in complete isolation, unable to
make contact with the outside world, in a place where
a man loses count of the days and where death can
strike in many ways. I had plenty of time to think,
but I tried not to. When a man loses his freedom,
thinking is a dangerous business—apt to drive him
mad. Eventually I was taken out and put in a cell with
other prisoners.'

Pain and disbelief streaked through Delphine at
the thought of what he had been subjected to. 'I am
sorry for the pain and indignities you must have been
forced to endure. Anyone who believes that revolution is a justifiable instrument of policy is a fool. It
is not something to be achieved in a day. Changes
have to be made gradually. To overturn the world is
to place the lower class at the top, but they will remain lower class.'

'That is so. These are troubled and dangerous times in France. The nobility, busy at the elaborate idleness in their grand chateaux or at the Palace of Versailles, in the swim of the gay life of Louis XVI's artificial paradise, should have seen this coming.'

'And now the King is dead and a new age has been born—a Republic of Liberty, Equality and Fraternity—and death for those who do not embrace it. I have no doubt Marie Antionette will suffer the same fate as her husband eventually. You were in the Conciergerie for twelve months. Why have they waited so long to take you to trial? Is it because you are English?'

'Being English makes no difference. English law means nothing here. I work for British Intelligence. What I was doing was highly confidential, therefore I am an enemy of the Republic with information that could be useful to them. When I was arrested I was involved in a plot to rescue the beleaguered King Louis. God alone knows how many foreign spies were loose in France at that time—and now, for that matter. I reckon I've had a narrow escape—for which I have you to thank.'

'I was following orders.'

'Of course you were, but you didn't have to. Why do you do it?'

'For the same reason as you yourself became a spy. I know very little about you, but I have been told that you completed impossible missions for the Intelligence Service before you were caught.'

'I like to think so. But what is it that drives you

to risk life and limb to save others? A noble act, I grant you, but it is a dangerous business—more so for a woman.'

'Sometimes being a woman can help. To portray oneself as a weak and silly girl, shallow and dim-witted who wouldn't know anything about anything, can often achieve things a man cannot. I cannot turn a blind eye to what is happening, so I help where I can.'

'You are under no obligation.'

'It is what I do—and I am rather good at it.' The smile she gave him as she turned her head away was not convincing.

'And I am full of admiration—and grateful,' he said with grave sincerity. 'I'm indebted to whatever reasons you had that made you appear at the Conciergerie. You have a mind of your own, I see.'

'Certainly. I should hardly be here doing what I do if I did not.'

'Nevertheless, it is a brave life you have chosen, saving aristocrats from the mob.'

'I don't discriminate. Jacques and I work together. Commoners or aristocrats—they are all the same to us. We do what we can to save people on merit, not their ancestry.'

'Of course you do, but it is not wise for one so young to walk such a dangerous tightrope.' His cool green eyes regarded her quizzically. 'What an extraordinary young woman you are. I would have thought young ladies could find more interesting and exciting ways of passing their time.'

As he gave her a long, leisurely look, there was

a twist of humour around his attractively moulded lips. The smile building about his mouth softened the hardness of his jaw and made him appear in that moment the most handsome man in the world to Delphine. Then, suddenly, his direct masculine assurance disconcerted her. She was acutely conscious of his close proximity to her and she felt an unfamiliar rush of blood singing through her veins. Instantly she felt resentment towards him. He had made too much of an impact on her and she was afraid that if he looked at her much longer he would read her thoughts with those brilliant clever eyes of his.

'I am sure you are right, but not nearly as rewarding or as worthwhile. What I do is more than a pastime for me. I see you are surprised.'

'Surprised, yes—and appalled to a certain extent. You are an attractive young woman and why your family has allowed you to become involved in this unusual and extremely dangerous occupation, I cannot imagine.'

Delphine's expression did not alter, but, stung by his words, something in her eyes stirred and hardened. 'As a rule I have never cared for anyone's opinion and I most certainly would never let them influence my actions. My work is often difficult and intense and frequently takes me away from home, but I take pride in what I do and what I achieve—that the people I help escape the terror if they're lucky. You would be surprised at the things I do—what I have seen. There is more than one kind of prison.'

'Do you work for the Intelligence Service?'

'I am not a spy—I realised I could do more for
those unfortunates than working out codes and wielding a knife, but if I pick something up I think is useful, I report back. British Intelligence have a team
that do this regularly. Not all are successful, but some
make it across the Channel. The network has loyal
people posing as supporters of the Republic—such
as Gaspard Ducat at the Conciergerie.'

'I thought he let me out for a heavy purse.'

'He did, but he also works for himself and not the
Republic.'

'It will be over one day—soon, I hope.'

'I would like to believe that, but life has taught me
such belief is fantasy, wishful thinking.'

'Nevertheless, it is a hard and dangerous life you
have chosen. Most young women would be having
fun attending parties and balls. You are so beautiful, young gentlemen would be dancing attendance
on you.'

She shook her head. 'I never was suited to wearing fine clothes and making small talk in society. I
would be bored out of my head for most of the time.'

He nodded. 'But you *are* beautiful. I suppose you
don't want to hear it—and not here in this place of
hopelessness—but all the same, it is true.'

Delphine knew she was beautiful. It was a fact.
She saw how men gazed at her with unabashed desire,
remarking on her eyes or her hair or her lips. This
Englishman saw her beauty in the gloomy light, but
he looked past it. Either that, or he was clever enough

to see that she wanted to offer more to the world than a beautiful face.

The smile she gave him was one of irony. 'You are right. I don't want to hear it. Not now. Not ever. I was meant for action—what I do suits me.'

'You have done well. You have saved many desperate souls—including my own. I shall be eternally grateful.'

Delphine slowly arched a brow and her smile was bland. 'So you should be. Your gratitude is something I appreciate. There are many more that will want saving before this is over. I shudder to think what will become of them all—what will become of France.'

'While ever the peasants starve and they continue to demand a fairer taxation system, France will not abolish the fight any time soon. Who gives you your instructions?'

'I take my orders from Sir Godfrey Bucklow at the Ministry of Defence. Have you heard of him?'

He nodded. 'I do know him. Sir Godfrey is a fine man, an exacting man—he must think highly of you to entrust you with such difficult tasks.'

'Being half-French, and because I speak the language fluently, he was delighted to use my services. He was the one who paired me up with Jacques. The three of us have good communication. It's worked well so far.'

'And the future? What does that hold for you?'

'I live for the present. Nothing more than that— and at this present time I must focus on getting you out of Paris.'

'Where are we headed?'

'I have orders to take you west to Granville.'

His eyes widened. 'Granville must be two hundred miles away.'

'If everything goes to plan, with little respite and changing the wagon outside Paris for a more serviceable equipage, which is waiting for us along with a change of clothes and provisions and horses en route, we should do it in two days.'

He raised an eyebrow. 'You have it arranged?'

'Oh, yes. Every step.'

'I'm impressed.'

'A vessel will be waiting to take us to Guernsey, which is where we will part company. You will meet someone there who will take you to London. But first we have to get out of Paris.'

'Through one of the gates.'

'It is the only way out. There are guards on every gate on the lookout for anything out of the ordinary—especially aristocrats fleeing Paris. Every day they uncover some fugitive royalist trying to flee the city and send them back to be tried by the tribunal. The guards are all revolutionaries who take it upon themselves to search everyone. It will be fraught with danger,'

'Why Guernsey? Why not go direct to Calais?'

'I am only following orders. But I think it is because now that Britain is at war with France, it will be safer. There is also a British fleet off the coast of Brittany. When your disappearance from the Conciergerie becomes known, Calais is the first place they will look.'

'And if the plan fails?'

As she got up from the table, Delphine's eyes were hard. 'It won't. I've made the journey several times. This time will be no different.' Walking towards the stairs in the corner of the room, she found it gave her courage to speak with an assured confidence, although the worst of the terror that had gripped her on going to the Conciergerie had left her. 'There is nothing we can do until morning so we might as well get some sleep. We have an early start and there will be no time for rest until we reach Granville. There is a small room up above if you would prefer. Maurice will show you should you wish.'

Rolling the cloak she had given him earlier into something resembling a cushion and placing it behind his head supported by the wall, then folding his arms across his chest, he shook his head. 'I'll stay where I am for the time being. Should we have any unwelcome visitors I have no wish to be caught napping.'

'As you like.'

Delphine paused with one foot on the bottom step of the stairs and looked back at him. When all the world was topsy-turvy, how could he simply close his eyes and go to sleep? She envied his inner calm. He had made quite an impression on her and was different to any man she had known. There was something sensuous about the manner in which he had regarded her, something, too, in the tone of his voice. She thought he was too much aware of her—

physically. He made her uneasy and yet at the same time he stimulated and excited her.

She told herself that he was nothing to her, just a handsome man she happened to rescue from his prison, and that as soon as they reached Guernsey any association between them would cease.

Laurence watched her toss her head, her plans made and confident they would be carried out successfully. He had considered telling her that now he was free of the Conciergerie he would make his own way to the coast, that to travel all the way to Granville was a bad idea, but thought better of it. She did not look like someone who would appreciate criticism, given or implied.

Making himself as comfortable as was possible, he thought of the young woman who was prepared to risk life and limb to get him out of France. All the while they had been talking she had studied him with cool interest, her expression immobile and guarded. His eyes had met her gaze and there were times when he thought she was looking into the heart of him, getting the measure of him, of his faults and failings. He had never seen eyes that contained more energy and depth.

It was not until he heard her voice that he realised the depth of her charm. Her voice was low, beautifully modulated, and her French was a joy to hear. Her face was softly rounded with a faint smattering of freckles. She had high cheekbones with a cream complexion and a perfect nose. Everything about her fas-

Chapter Two

By morning the rain had abated and the day dawned sultry and warm. Delphine found the Englishman waiting for her, impatient for them to be on their way. He was lounging in his chair, the very image of relaxed elegance with his long legs stretched out in front of him. He rose to his feet and slowly advanced towards her with a graceful ease surprising in a man of such virile appearance.

'We will leave shortly,' she said, 'as soon as you are dressed for the journey.'

He stared at her in amazement, one eyebrow cocked. The voice was clearly the woman who had secreted him from the Conciergerie, but her appearance did not fit the description. Her skirts and blouse were those of a peasant woman, her hair tucked beneath a brown wig that straggled about her face untidily. A well-worn floppy hat sat atop her head, sporting a tricolour. She looked at him, raising an eyebrow.

'What?'

He chuckled softly. 'I'm lost for words.'

'I know how I must look—I don't cut a pretty fig-ure. Get used to it. This is how it has to be. It wouldn't do for me to pass through the gate looking like a lady. I'd be arrested on the spot.' She tossed him a bundle of clothes. 'And don't look so smug,' she said, smil-ing coolly. 'You will look no better when we have you ready to take your place in the wagon. Put those on and burn the clothes you are wearing. They stink of the Conciergerie.'

He laughed softly. 'Your disguise is perfect—but I suspect that beneath it all is a fiery, raving beauty that one would want to run off with.'

'I wouldn't bet on it,' she quipped. 'Now change your clothes. I'll go and see Jacques while you change.'

Leaving through a door that led to a yard where Jacques was waiting with the wagon, she was not thinking of her appearance—she seldom did, but his comment had planted a tiny seed in her mind: the be-ginning of consciousness that, regardless of her cho-sen occupation, she was still a woman beneath it all.

'Have you everything ready, Jacques?'

He nodded. 'I'll leave you to it. I'll stay with my brother and his family here in Paris for a few days before making my way back to Guernsey.' Concern for her safety was evident in his eyes. 'Have a care. Take no chances and have a safe journey.'

When Delphine returned to the tavern the English-man had changed into the poor-quality clothes he was to wear for the journey. Wielding a pen with a small pot of paint, she told him to sit down.

'You will be in the back of the wagon, my brother—who I will assure the guards is at death's door, that you have the pox. It is my hope that no one will dare approach you. But you must play your part. A few groans and shivers here and there will not go amiss.'

He frowned. 'You have papers to show the guard?'

She nodded. 'If necessary. After that I have another set of papers for us both should we be apprehended. You will be Citizen Claude Blanchard and I will pass as your wife, Sophie.'

'And my trade? I do have one?'

'You are a wine merchant travelling to Rennes in Brittany on business and to visit relatives. We must converse in French at all times. Consequences could be dire if we are heard speaking English. We are both fluent in French—but there is an occasional betrayal which gives you away so have a care—so if we are stopped, hopefully no one will suspect we are anything other than what we seem. Do not forget that if they know you have escaped the Conciergerie, then they will be looking for an Englishman. Memorise your assumed name if you will. When we have left Paris we will stop and dress in plain clothes as befits a man and his wife of modest means. Good clothes are enough to brand a person, as the mob attribute fine dress to nobles and rich bourgeois. Now please sit down so that I can apply some spots to your face.'

Mutely he obeyed. She moved to stand before him,

her eyes riveted on his face. He had no objection to what she was about to do—in fact, he appeared to welcome her closeness.

'Have you done this before?' he asked conversationally.

'No, this is the first time. We usually devise something to cause a distraction, but this is the first time we've used the pox. It was Jacques's idea. Hopefully it will keep the guards at bay and let us through. Not all those we help come through Paris, which is easier for us. Jacques will not be coming with us. He has family here in Paris he is concerned about—a brother and his family. Now please sit still. I have to make them look authentic.'

'Then I am yours to command and surrender myself to your ministering completely.' He chuckled.

Amazed by his unflappable calm, Delphine began to perform her task with as little contact as possible between them. Conscious of his nearness, with a militant look in her eyes she tipped his head back with her finger and began to apply the spots carefully to the lean contours of his face.

'You have a steady hand,' he murmured. 'I pray it doesn't rain and wash away the spots before we reach the gate.'

'In which case you will have to cover your face.'

Preoccupied with her task and gnawing on her bottom lip in deep concentration as she carefully dabbed the paint on his brow, she tried not to ponder the magnetic pull of the man, the look of those penetrating eyes. A smile curved his lips as he studied her face at such close quarters—he was clearly relishing her ministrations. How could he have made such an impact on her? The light in the depths of his eyes as he watched her closely was as enigmatic as it was challenging and, unexpectedly, she felt a quiver of excitement.

The quickening in his eyes told her he was aware of that response. She paused in her task and frowned irately when he shuffled forward to be closer to her. The movement shocked her to the depths of her virginal innocence and made her heart pound in her chest.

'Please sit still. I think you're beginning to enjoy this. Do you have to sit so close? Sit back,' she ordered, meeting the enigmatic gaze of the man who was perhaps nine years older than her in years but centuries older than her in experience, who had done and seen everything there was to do and see and who knew exactly the effect his closeness was having on her.

Her prim reprimand brought a smile to his lips. 'Have you applied sufficient spots? You must ensure they look convincing. Are you confident we will get through the gate without being apprehended?'

'I wouldn't be doing this if I wasn't confident that I can do it.'

'No, I don't believe you would. I'm beginning to realise you are no ordinary young lady—a dark horse if ever there was is how I would describe you—clever and cunning, and dangerous to know,' he said quietly, his gaze levelled on her face. 'A woman after my own heart.'

Delphine met his gaze and paused with the brush between them. 'Oh, no, Claude Blanchard,' she said coolly. 'You can keep your heart. That is the last thing I want from you.'

He regarded her long and hard before replying, 'I shall. My heart has always been in my own safekeeping and there it will remain. Safe. But you intrigue me, Sophie Blanchard. Already I am wondering what I have let myself in for.'

'You'll have to wait to find out.' Delphine began again, oddly relaxed by the low timbre of his voice and the steadiness of his gaze. Having covered most of his face, she paused to gaze at her handiwork, studying his face. She saw arrogance in the jut of his jaw and an indomitable pride and strength etched in every finely moulded feature. She was also beginning to sense a powerful charisma that had nothing to do with his handsome looks and powerful physique, or that mocking smile of his and brilliant flashing eyes.

Deciding it was prudent to change to a more serious subject, they went over the broad outline of their plan. It was an audacious one and the Englishman's eyes were occasionally shadowed with doubt when they discussed how difficult it would be getting through the gate. In Delphine's eyes there was never anything but confidence that was so infectious that he soon abandoned every objection, putting all his trust in her.

She focused her attention on applying the few remaining spots, eager to complete her task so she could

move away, for she was aware of a gnawing disquiet
settling on her at being too close for too long. Somewhere deep within her a spark flickered and flared,
setting her skin ablaze and filling her body with liquid fire. Despite her rioting nerves, outwardly she
remained calm.

'Hold still,' she murmured. 'I'm almost finished.'

A slow smile curved his lips. 'Are you sure you
have the stomach for what we are about to do?'

A rueful smile brought up the corners of her lips.
'I have a cast-iron stomach.'

When she had finished she stood back to survey
her handiwork. 'There. You do look convincing—I
only hope we can convince the guards on the gate
and they do not look too closely. Now come along.
We must be away.'

After paying the landlord his due, they went to
the waiting wagon.

The Englishman gave the horse a disapproving
look. 'The horse is a sorry-looking nag. Will it get
us to where we are going?'

'It's stronger than it looks. It will suffice until we
have put Paris behind us and we change to something
more suitable.'

Grim and determined on getting out of Paris, Delphine climbed on top and took up the reins. They
were not apprehended as the wagon trundled through
the busy streets towards the west gate. The traffic was
a slow-moving mass of wagons and peasants shuffling towards the lofty gate. Delphine felt her nerves
tighten the closer they got. Up ahead the guards were

closely inspecting wagons and pulling apart goods for a thorough examination. There was a disturbance up ahead when a carriage was searched and an elderly man and woman were found concealed in the back. Soon the people milling about the gate were shouting, *'Aristos—death to aristos!'*

From where she waited further down the line, Delphine broke out into the icy sweat of fear, feeling the damp on her back. As they neared the impressive gate another wagon full of casks was stopped and searched. Delphine turned and told the Englishman to enact a fever. His green eyes sparkled up at her and his mouth stretched in an audacious grin.

'I have every faith that you will get us through, but I will do my utmost to assist you.'

One of the guards ordered them to halt. Delphine pulled the horse to a stop and leaned over to speak to the guard.

'What have you in the back?' he demanded, not too friendly, his manner surly.

'Not much. Take a look—you'll find my brother— poorly he is,' Delphine said, making a play of scratching her shoulder as the guard moved closer to take a look. The man in the back was tossing and muttering incoherently, his eyes rolling back in their sockets, his face covered with the telltale spots of the pox. 'Think it's the pox so I wouldn't get too close.'

As soon as she mentioned the word *pox* the guard took a backward step. 'Where are you taking him?'

'Home—to his farm near Corbevoie. Been off it for

a couple of days, he has—then this morning the spots. Let his wife take care of him, I said.'

'If he lives that long,' the guard grumbled.

'Aye—well—there is that. How much longer, I say?'

Another of his fellow guards came to join him. When he would have approached the wagon his fellow guard pulled him back.

'Don't—he's pox-ridden. I've seen it myself.'

The guard immediately paled and his eyes filled with fear. The wagons and citizens behind began to pull back. The dreaded plague aroused fear and disgust in everyone.

The guard waved them on, eager for them to be gone. 'Move on, damn you—and take your wretched pox with you.'

Delphine didn't need telling twice. Flicking the reins, she urged the horse on, the wagon bouncing its occupant none too gently in the back. Not until they were well away from the city did she slow the wagon.

'Morbleu!' came a low-sounding voice. 'My admiration for you grows by the minute.' He chuckled. 'But it's too rich. The clever English spy laid low by a dose of the pox. How can this be happening, I ask myself—and to me, of all people? For shame. There is no justice in the world.'

Delphine found herself laughing as the tension that had gripped her as they'd passed through the gate diminished slightly. 'Don't think of getting up yet,' she said, turning and looking down into his glittering eyes. 'There's still a way to go so we must be on our guard—it is possible that we are being watched.

You could close your eyes and feign sleep—or even go to sleep if you so wish.'

He heaved a sigh and gave her a hazy-eyed stare. 'I find I like your orders. What sane man would question them? But it would seem I have exchanged one kind of tyranny for another. Sophie Blanchard—or whoever you are—you are incorrigible.'

'Yes, I know. Do you mind?'

Despite the seriousness of their situation, he laughed out loud. 'Not a bit. In fact, I suddenly find myself looking forward to our journey together. It will be interesting to see which of us will have expired before the journey's end.'

Delphine laughed and looked ahead, relieved to see the traffic thinning out. 'I'm a woman on a mission, Englishman, and I will not be deterred from the task allotted to me.'

As the wagon rattled through the Normandy countryside, Delphine felt a great relief at leaving Paris behind. They drove to a posting house, one Delphine had used on occasion. Here they ate a hurried meal and changed clothes into something more in keeping with a wine merchant and his wife. They abandoned the wagon in favour of a hired four-wheeled travelling chaise which was small and discreet, with no outward signs of wealth beyond a pair of post horses which they would change at regular intervals.

Coach travel could be long and tedious and virtually impossible during the winter months when days were short and some of the roads became impassable.

But with the long summer days, frequent changes of horses enabled many miles to be covered.

Relieved to have something to do, the Englishman took the reins and urged the horses into a fast trot, clicking the reins smartly. Delphine sat beside him as they sped along, travelling through open countryside, rolling green fields and woods and the occasional village with windmills and cottages huddled together.

When they were settled, the Englishman glanced across at Delphine. 'I am aware that you carry a couple of pistols beneath your skirts. I saw them at the inn.'

'We have a long journey ahead of us and, if we are to travel through the night, it's as well that we have protection. In these troubled times all manner of threats roam the countryside—miscreants, cutthroats, ruthless thugs and soldiers—the latter we must avoid.'

'I agree. Do you really know how to fire a pistol?' he enquired.

'I happen to be a crack shot.'

'Now why am I not surprised?'

When it came to defending herself, her father had taught Delphine all she needed to know about firearms, which had been a proviso Sir Godfrey had insisted upon before agreeing to recruit her.

They had travelled throughout the day and night, taking turns to drive the chaise so the other could rest inside. With their minds constantly alert and set on putting as much distance between them and Paris, they had taken to the back roads so as to avoid drawing attention to themselves, only stopping at post inns to change the horses. It was midday when the Englishman pulled into a wooded area to take a brief rest.

'It's going to be another long night. And,' he said, looking at the gathering thunder clouds overhead, 'I think we might be in for a storm. We should take respite and eat while we can.'

Leaving the horses to nibble at the grass and carrying a small basket of food, they sought shelter in the trees. Sunlight filtered through the branches and loose twigs crunched beneath their feet. The air was sultry and smelled of woodland decay. The Englishman lowered himself to the ground and began to unpack the food before leaning back against the stout trunk of a tree, adjusting his back to the rough bark. Delphine watched him, feeling quite relaxed and at ease. Lowering herself to the ground, she smoothed her skirts that had risen to reveal her shapely shins above her boots. Glancing to her right, she caught the look in his eyes which watched her every move. They were as sharp as a needle point and revealed a kind of clarified hunger—a hunger not for food, she realised as he slowly turned away.

They shared crusty bread, a wedge of cheese and apples. At any other time this small meal would have been enjoyed in a haze of sunshine and warm contentment, and they would talk and laugh. But until they were safe aboard the ship which would take them to Guernsey, the tension inside them both was too great.

Having eaten their fill, they sat in companionable silence for a while.

'Do you intend returning to France in the near future?' the Englishman asked at length.

Delphine sighed, shaking her head slowly. In the dim light his face appeared pale and shadowed. 'If I am needed, I will. There are a lot of people who have come together, wanting to help those in grave danger in France. The people at the top mobilise individuals like me.'

'Is it worth it? Do you not think you should stop before anything happens to you—before you forget there are such things as being a young lady, of laughing and doing things that hold no danger?'

Her expression tightened and her slender body was rigid, as if her anger was barely confined by good sense. 'No, I haven't thought of it. At this time I have no choice. It's this or nothing.'

'You're trading your youth for a dangerous game. You have been fortunate so far—but even in your darkest hours you must have your doubts. Who knows of your involvement?'

'No one—and I mean no one.'

'Your family?'

'I have precious little family left.'

'Someone must miss you.'

She smiled. 'I have become creative in explaining my absences.'

'And if something should happen to you?'

'I have learned my lesson in survival as diligently as I studied mathematics and other subjects as a child.

And what of you? Will you return to your occupation as a government agent—which you were rather good at according to Sir Godfrey.'

He smiled crookedly. 'I've had my fill of France for the time being. Besides, I have commitments that will be demanding my attention at home.'

'Yes, I expect you have. Because of what you do, would I be right in assuming there is no wife waiting for you at home?'

'You would. I am not married—although with two older sisters happily ensconced with husbands and children, when I return they will no doubt press me to enter that respectable institution to produce an heir eventually.'

'Oh, dear. You don't sound enthusiastic.'

'Enthusiastic or not, it is something I will have to give serious thought to.'

'I think I know exactly the kind of woman you will marry.'

'You do? Tell me—I am all ears.'

'Very well. I imagine you will marry and settle down with a woman who will preside over your fine house with grace and poise, a woman who has been trained to manage the demanding responsibilities of such a house and provide you with an heir to carry on your name.'

He laughed. 'You have a remarkable imagination, Sophie.'

'But I am right.' He nodded. 'Then it is evident to me that you are thinking with your head and not your heart, that you consider marriage with the same kind of dispassion and practised precision you would employ when dealing with business transactions.'

He shrugged. 'Did you expect anything else? Most marriages are business arrangements—arranged for convenience. Why should I imagine mine will be any different?'

'But surely a man would want to like his wife? After all, they have to spend a lifetime together.'

'A poor man will put up with a woman in exchange for her money.'

'And is that what you are? A poor man?'

A tight smile hovered on his firm lips. 'My financial affairs were looking bleak when I left London. I doubt things have changed. I am no more sentimental about marriage than anyone else. It's a contract like any other.'

'I am aware that it is the law that everything a wife possesses when she marries becomes the property of her husband, to dispose of as he sees fit. If that is the kind of marriage you seek, then you can expect your marriage to be excruciatingly boring. Marriage is not a business transaction.'

'No? And what are your views on marriage? I am interested to hear them.'

'I feel that where something as important as marriage is concerned, then it is essential that the two people concerned love each other.'

He smiled. 'In my opinion, that is sentimental nonsense. Among society, it is considered unfashionable for husbands and wives to spend all their waking days together. But what of you? Do you have commitments at home, Sophie?'

She swallowed down the sadness that swept over her. 'My family has been irreparably broken by the revolution. I was not in France when I heard that my aunt and my uncle had been taken—' her voice shook slightly, but she swallowed hard and carried on '—along with my father.'

Sympathy flickered in the Englishman's eyes. 'I'm so sorry.'

'Yes. An overwhelming sense of loss consumed me when I heard this. I tried to imagine what they had gone through. I felt so helpless. They went the way of others of aristocratic birth—to the guillotine. At this present time the life of a noble is not worth a candle in France.'

Like everyone else, Delphine knew all about Dr Guillotin's newly invented machine for beheading victims, which was meant to spare them needless pain—and instead he had created a monster. The new Republic considered the contraption to be a real social advance—democracy in action—but its efficiency meant an increase in the severed heads of innocent victims, from tens to hundreds a week.

'I know they went to the guillotine—but I do not know what has happened to my father. I do not know if he is dead or alive, but I will not give up on him. I have to know what has happened to him. He was arrested with my aunt and uncle and taken to Paris. Nothing has been heard of him since then. He either escaped or is languishing in one of Paris's infamous prisons.'

'And naturally you are anxious to discover what happened to him. You are right. The matter cannot be dismissed lightly. Have you tried to resolve the mystery?'

She nodded. 'I have done nothing else. Sir Godfrey is aware of my situation and has agents in Paris seeking information. No one has been able to come up with anything. Every time I help someone escape the terror it lifts me out of the darkness of losing my family, always giving me a reason to smile and be thankful—and I live in hope that someone will be able to tell me what happened to my father.'

Falling silent and feeling hot tears scald her eyes, she averted her gaze. The carefully constructed dam around her heart had held for three years. For a moment, as they talked, the Englishman had broken through the shell of reserve she had learned to erect around herself.

Since beginning her forays into France she'd witnessed despicable atrocities and never shed a tear and she wouldn't do so now—not in front of this stranger. Swallowing her tears, she looked at him with defiance, hoping he would see how much what had happened to her family and the revolution had toughened her. He'd see how thick her skin was and that she really did have ice in her veins.

'I'm so sorry.'

She shrugged. 'Thank you. It happened and now it's over.'

'It isn't, though, is it? Not for you?'

She searched his eyes which, at that moment,

seemed to pierce her soul. 'No,' she replied quietly. 'No, it isn't.'

They sat in silence, each preoccupied with their own thoughts. Delphine glanced across to where the Englishman sat. She watched as he swept his hair that had fallen over his brow back with his long fingers. She found her eyes drawn to the action and to his face. Never more conscious of this sudden weakness, she dragged her eyes away and fixed her attention on the trees beyond, feeling all kinds of guilt. The Englishman closed his eyes, folding his arms across his chest, blissfully ignorant about having been the unwitting source of any turmoil within her.

It was when she had got to her feet and was about to collect their provisions that Delphine heard a sound coming from deeper in the woods. She was startled, too startled to be afraid at first. Turning, she looked at her companion who had risen to his feet. He, too, had heard the sound. His face was grim as he peered into the dense woodland.

'What's wrong?' she whispered, following his gaze, her whole body alert to danger.

'I'm not sure.'

Again a sound—a rustling of leaves. The Englishman looked like a different person. The amiable rogue was gone, replaced by a sober man, his face grim and hard, his eyes fierce.

'Get behind me,' he ordered.

'What—'

'Do as I say and give me one of those pistols,' he snapped when she looked as if she were about to argue.

Delphine obeyed, darting behind him and peering ahead to watch, her heart pounding, her finger on the trigger of the other pistol which she drew from beneath her skirts. The sound of rustling came closer. A moment later the head of a young deer appeared and then the rest of it, before taking one look at them and scampering back into the woodland.

The Englishman chucked softly. 'Well, I'll be!'

Delphine was so relieved she almost fell. Grinning, the Englishman placed his arm about her to steady her. She clung to him a moment, savouring his strength. He held her against him, smiling, a lazy, satisfied smile as he captured her eyes.

'I'll be damned if you aren't the most bewitching creature I've seen in a long time.'

She pushed herself away. 'That might have something to do with you being locked up for the past twelve months,' she quipped, trying to sound all prim and proper while her insides were melting from his nearness.

He laughed, gathering up their basket. 'Why, for one moment I thought you were—'

She flushed hotly, knowing exactly what he was about to say and stopping him. 'I wasn't,' she retorted firmly. 'Nothing was further from my mind. Now come along. Enough time has been wasted.'

'Do you think so?' His warm green eyes were merry.

'Yes—although I have to admit that you're quite handy to have around,' she remarked, turning her back on him.

'I reckon I am,' he admitted. 'A woman could do worse.'

She looked at him. He was like a different person when he laughed. His eyes were brilliant, full of laughter. His mouth had changed, too. It had softened. 'I imagine she could.'

Slinging the basket over his arm, he chuckled softly. 'Now come, Wife. We'd best get a move on.'

His eyes twinkled wickedly and Delphine looked at him sharply. 'Only for the duration of the journey,' she retorted, quick to resent his easy manner, yet despite her attempt to remain cool and detached, her heart beat out an uncontrollable rhythm of excitement. She stalked on ahead of him, unable to believe the impudence of the man, but then she smiled, strangely enjoying his teasing and seeing the funny side of the incident, and the relief they had both felt when the young deer appeared from the forest.

For a moment she realised she was content to have this man beside her, warm, friendly and comforting. He was strong and considerate, which had proved to be the case when he'd taken charge of the situation— there was tenderness there, too. The surprise intrusion of the deer had been a light-hearted moment, easing the tension they both felt, if just for a moment, yet it was a moment that had brought her the kind of relaxation she had not known for a long time. However, she realised that some caution should perhaps be observed in future.

'I hope you don't harbour an aversion to being

alone with me for such a lengthy period,' the Englishman said, taking her hand to assist her into the chaise.

'Why should I?' Delphine enquired quizzically,
pausing with her foot on the step to look at him. 'Unless, of course, you are a rogue at heart.'

'I may well be,' the Englishman acknowledged,
lifting to his lips the slender fingers of his assumed
wife, letting his warm mouth linger on her knuck-
les in a slow, sensual caress. 'Will you sit with me
on top?'

Aware of a strange quivering in the pit of her body
when his lips came into contact with her skin, she de-
clined. 'I think I'll be safer inside for the time being.'
Sliding her hand from his, she lifted her skirts to
step aboard and immediately felt her companion's
hand beneath her elbow aiding her ascent. She settled herself on the seat while striving to control her
composure.

His eyes danced teasingly up into hers, his lips
curved into a smile. 'Fear not—I shall take care to
treat you as I would a wife—with the utmost respect.'

As Delphine listened to the warm and mellow tone
of his voice, and her gaze lit upon the handsomely
chiselled visage, her eyes were drawn into the snare
and for a moment she found herself susceptible to the
appeal of that wondrous smile.

When he'd left her and the chaise moved off, Delphine relaxed back in her seat. When they had shared
their simple fare she had found herself colouring as
she looked up suddenly and caught his warm unabashed gaze on her—he had looked at her as a man

looks at a woman he finds attractive and desirable. He hadn't tried to conceal that look or turn it into anything less than what it was. She had been the one to lower her eyes. The moment had passed, but the memory of it stayed with her.

Strangely, being with the Englishman gave her a certain feeling of security, for although the encounter with the deer had passed off as nothing to be alarmed about, she could not rid herself of the fear and apprehension that they would encounter trouble before the journey was over.

Chapter Three

Darkness had fallen when the weather turned suddenly. The clouds burst and rain began to pour down relentlessly. The wind rose, becoming strong. As luck would have it they were close to a coaching inn. As they pulled into the yard, with no let-up in the rain, Delphine suggested they stay the night, setting off again at first light. To continue with their journey while the storm was raging would be foolhardy.

The general air inside the inn was one of comfort. There were just a few patrons, some of them eating. Delphine and the Englishman sat in an alcove next to the hearth, which offered them a little privacy. The acrid odour of ale and the appetising aroma of hot food pervaded every corner and started Delphine's mouth watering. The food was good and they attacked it with relish.

Feeling the dampness beginning to leave her bones and a tiredness wrapping itself around her, Delphine had not realised until then the depth of her fatigue.

Patrons began to drift to their rooms and her thoughts turned to her own predicament—that of sharing a room with the Englishman.

Gazing into the glowing heart of the fire when he left her to have a word with the landlord, she was content to bask in the warmth and closed her eyes. She was brought back to awareness when a face loomed close and a hand reached out for her. Immediately she was alert, thrusting the arm away from her.

'Don't... Oh! It's you, Claude. I—I thought...' She sighed. 'I don't know what I thought?'

'That I posed a threat, obviously,' he retorted drily. 'I'm sorry I startled you. You're tired. It's time to retire. The landlady will show you to our room. I'll be up shortly.'

Without a word Delphine picked up her bag containing a few necessary items and followed the landlady up the rickety stairs. Sharing a room with her supposed husband was something she had hoped to avoid. The room was warm and she could feel perspiration on her back and between her breasts. Sitting on the bed, she removed her boots, pushing her hair back from her face with the back of her hand impatiently, wishing that her fingers were not so damp and her mind so active. Hoping her companion would linger down below over his ale, she slipped out of her dress and dipped her hands into the cool water.

Entering the chamber sooner than Delphine had expected, Laurence paused a moment to take in the sight that greeted him. It made him catch his breath.

She had removed her dress and her arms and shoulders were bare, her thick golden tresses trailing down her back in wild confusion. Rubbing soap on to her creamy skin, she was so absorbed in her task that she was unaware of his presence. Utterly bewitched and enchanted he stood perfectly still, unable to drag his eyes away from this treasure that was indeed a sight for sore eyes. Everything about her was untamed and every move she made was a sensual invitation to his starved senses.

What little there was of her shift moulded itself to her body with endearing delight and his eyes devoured the loveliness she displayed, every nerve in his body coming alive and responding to her as she leaned over the bowl to wash her face. His gaze followed tiny droplets of water as they trickled slowly down her throat and disappeared between the curves of her fully ripened breasts, their roundness and rosy peaks invitingly exposed and beckoning his hungry gaze as her skimpy white bodice scooped open to reveal all.

Unwittingly, he must have made a sound, or she sensed his presence, for with a gasp she turned towards the door swiftly, placing the towel in front of her to conceal her nakedness. Her eyes widened with furious rage when they focused on his unsmiling face. She flushed scarlet, but then her chin came up and she burst into life like an erupting volcano.

'Claude Blanchard!' she lambasted. 'Have you no manners at all that you must come prowling and spy on me?'

'I beg your pardon,' he said, swiftly turning so his back was facing her. 'The door was off the latch and, seeing how fatigued you were, I thought perhaps you might have gone to bed.'

'Couldn't you have taken a while longer over your ale? A little privacy would not go amiss.' She spoke scathingly. 'Your forward behaviour is—is not—proper.'

'Proper?' He laughed softly. 'We're a long way from propriety and protocol and all that nonsense that governs one's life in London. Here, in our own bedchamber, it doesn't count.'

'Not to you, maybe, but it does to me.'

Despite the stubborn lift to her chin and her rebellious tone, there was a tremor of fear in her voice and when Laurence heard it he became still. Since beginning the journey, she had shown so much indefatigable spirit that he'd actually believed nothing could shake her. Remembering the faint blue smudges beneath her glorious eyes, he realised that the ordeal of her assignment affected her deeply. She was amazing, he thought—extremely brave and determined as hell.

'Fear not, Sophie,' he said, moving to the bed and sitting down to remove his boots, still with his back to her. 'I shall not abuse or take advantage of you in your moment of weakness. I will try to restrain myself, difficult as that will be while ever we are together.'

Resting back against the pillows, he closed his eyes, unable to suppress the memory of his companion's adorable assets. The longer they were together, the more he became attracted to her. He wondered about the allure, for it was more than her face and body that drew him to her. She had a presence that warmed him, a fiery spirit that challenged him.

On a more serious note, he knew he must fight to keep tight rein on his desires where she was concerned. He was in no position to form a serious relationship with a woman at this time. He was plagued by an awareness of an emptiness in his life. Because of his work with the Intelligence Service, which sent him away for long periods with the added fact that his life could be cut short at any time, marriage was an uneasy subject he ignored. But he could not ignore the fact that with his finances depleted, at this present time he had very precious little to offer any woman.

After a long angry moment and seeing Claude had his back to her on the bed, Delphine calmed down enough to finish her toilet. Tentatively she turned back the feather comforter on the bed and crept between the sheets, settling herself as near to the edge as it was possible without falling out.

Turning on her side, she lay there, listening to him breathe as he fell to sleep, furious with herself. It was ridiculous that she was lying there with a man who was a stranger to her. It was idiotic of her to have suggested they spent the night at the inn—she was now of the opinion that a wet night on the open road would have been preferable to this. But here she was and there was not a thing she could do about it.

But considering what had just passed between them, she was beginning to realise that she was not as immune to her companion's magnetism as she had thought. When she had turned and seen him standing there, his mere presence seeming to fill the small chamber, for a brief moment she had been overcome with a feeling of excitement and anticipation, which she had soon quashed.

Because he was fully dressed, she had been extremely conscious of her own state of undress. She was also conscious and alarmed that she was stirred by his masculinity. But refusing to surrender to the call of her blood, she had crushed these treacherous feelings that threatened to weaken her and taken refuge in anger and indignation instead.

Laurence awoke to the sound of the inn stirring to life. Turning his head, he took a moment to look at the young woman who had rolled close to his side in her sleep. What a glorious creature she was. Her lips were moist and parted slightly, the thick crescent of her lashes sweeping her cheeks, hiding the deep, warm amber of her eyes. Long tendrils of her golden hair were spread on the pillow. He watched the slow rise and fall of her chest. Still attired in her chemise, the thought of all her soft, warm flesh beneath was causing his imagination to run wild.

Something in his heart moved and softened, then something stabbed him in the centre of his chest. What the hell was wrong with him? She was on an assignment to get him out of France and he was grateful to her, yet at the same time he was overwhelmed by the realisation that, if he didn't take care, she would come to mean something to him—and he wasn't ready for that.

Sophie Blanchard was an unusual female, intelligent, opinionated and full of surprises. She was also the epitome of stubborn, prideful woman. Yet for all her fire and spirit, there was no underlying viciousness. He found himself wondering about the woman behind the mask, the woman who kept her secret, innermost feelings carefully concealed and faced the world with a defiant show of strength and pride. The image she showed to the world was that she was unbreakable, that she had a steel exterior, but he suspected it protected a soft heart.

She was so very different from the sophisticated, worldly women he had taken to bed in the past—experienced, sensual women, knowledgeable in the ways of love, women who knew how to please him. This young woman was different, a phenomenon. He sensed a goodness in her, something special, sensitive—something worth pursuing. There was also something untapped inside her that not even she was aware of—passion buried deep. What would happen if she allowed it all to come out? In sleep she looked so innocent. He was dangerously fascinated by this vulnerable side to her, he realised, and settled down to observe her sleeping profile a moment longer, reluctant to wake her. Nothing made sense, for nothing could explain why he was beginning to enjoy being alone with her.

* * *

On waking, Delphine turned her head to find herself looking into the Englishman's drowsy, half-closed eyes. He was on his side, leaning on his elbow and looking down at her. Immediately she was fully awake and rolled away from him. She had been lying on her side, her head resting on his upper arm, her body pressed far too closely against the length of his.

'You might have wakened me,' she chided, swinging her legs off the bed and reaching for her dress. 'It is daylight already. Hopefully we'll be able to get something to eat before we leave.'

Sitting on the edge of the bed, Claude pulled on his boots and went to the door. 'I'll leave you to dress while I order breakfast and perhaps have some food packed up for the journey.'

The rain had ceased and the sky was clear of cloud when they resumed their journey. After what seemed to be an eternity they were approaching Granville. A lightening of spirits seemed to come over them both. Seated on top of the chaise beside Claude, Delphine looked ahead and smelled the salty kiss of the sea on the wind. Dusk had fallen with a soft pink haze by the time they entered the town.

'The boat will be waiting,' she said, her attention fixed on the busy harbour. 'It's a fishing vessel—*The Seagull*—and often puts in at Granville so it will not attract attention from the coastguard. Have you ever been to Guernsey?'

'No—although I know it's favoured by the smuggling fraternity. Tobacco, brandy and tea and other commodities—smuggled goods—pass through the island from France to be bought by the men along the coast of England, uncaring that they break the law by not paying customs duty on them.'

Delphine laughed. 'Yes, that's true—they also make fortunes—and woe betide any man who informs on them. His life wouldn't be worth living.'

'I suspect his life would be snuffed out. You are quite right, Sophie—or whoever you are—there is money to be made from smuggling—a lot of money.'

She gave him a quizzical look. 'Why, what is this? Are you considering a change in occupation, perhaps? Although the dangers to smugglers can be as great as they are to a spy.'

He grinned. 'True—but I find the adventure of it appealing.'

Delphine didn't deign to question further—his manner told her he spoke in jest, but she suspected there was more than a little truth behind his words.

Darkness had fallen when they entered the town. Despite the late hour the quay was bustling with activity, cargo being loaded and unloaded by the light of lanterns hanging along the quay and from the rigging of vessels, glowing like fireflies.

Their vessel was waiting and, after leaving the chaise at a posting house, they were watched aboard by John Fletcher, the skipper himself. He was not tall and by no means young, but he was still a fine figure of a man. His grey canvas shirt was open to the waist, revealing the hard muscles of his chest. His eyes were dark and brilliant and the black hair that sprang from under a tilted black cap was streaked with silver.

'Are we late, John? We've made good time.'

'You have. I was late putting in—the wind was against us—but I had to come to pick up my favourite spy.'

'I'm not a spy—as well you know,' she said, walking with him to the rails. 'I merely do what I can, when I can to rescue certain citizens from losing their heads.'

'And this latest? You managed to get him out of the Conciergerie, I see—at no small risk to yourself. You're a brave lass. You've done well.'

She nodded, looking to where the Englishman was coming aboard. 'How long before we can be away?'

'As soon as the fish has been unloaded. The tide's with us so we should be away within half an hour. Who is he anyway?'

'I know him as Claude Blanchard, but that isn't his real name. He's a British agent and that's all I know about him.'

'Didn't you think to ask?'

'I try not to think too much. Besides, it's best not to know too much.'

'Must be important for the powers that be to go to such lengths to arrange his escape from the Conciergerie.'

'Yes, I suppose he is—but as for saving anyone else… I have commitments at home. This may well be my last trip for a while.'

'You should make it permanent. It's not right for a young woman to be risking life and limb.'

'No—well… I have my grandfather to think of. He's not well.'

'And your aunt?'

'Great-Aunt Amelia.'

'They're still not speaking, I take it?'

'No—they haven't spoken for years.' She grinned. 'Truth to tell, John, I think they enjoy being at loggerheads. Aunt Amelia is eighty-six years old, but anyone would think she was in her prime the way she bustles about and orders everyone to do her bidding.'

'Aye, well, neither of them is getting any younger and you have your future to think of—now you can no longer make your home in France.'

'I know that, John. I am of an age where I know marriage is the destiny of all women and, because of what has happened to my family in France, my destiny is foremost in my grandfather's mind.'

Sails flapped above Laurence as he felt the salt wind ruffle his hair. The crew ran about the deck and the skipper was at the tiller. As soon as the vessel left the French shore, the tension he had been under for longer than he cared to remember began to recede. Even his companion, standing with the skipper, looked more at ease with herself and seemed to breathe more freely.

Suddenly the sails swelled as they caught a gust of wind and he breathed in deeply with sudden exhilaration. The wind smacked of freedom, of England and home. During his imprisonment it was what he had dreamed about, and now, as he felt the wind on his face, it came to him suddenly that there was a fierce joy in severing all ties with France. Impulsively he threw back his head and laughed, as if he were offering himself up to be carried away by it.

His laughter brought his companion to come and stand beside him, to look up at him in fascination and curiosity. Their eyes met and held and something in that moment passed between them. Deep within himself he had to admit that a flame had been ignited that in time could burst into a fierce fire. It was absurd to feel that way about a perfect stranger and in such dire circumstances, but he could not help it.

'You are glad to be going home,' she said.

'Absolutely,' he said, still laughing. 'I love the sea and I love the wind that will drive me on. I am happy I am going home. I never thought I would see the day.' Tearing his eyes from the sea, he looked down at her. 'And you? If you decide not to return, I suspect you will miss France.'

'I miss the old France and everything that was familiar to me. I don't know what happened to my home—if it is still standing. If not, then it is a terrible shame. It was where I was born. It was one of the finest and oldest chateaux in that part of the country—in the Auvergne region, the home of my father's family for centuries and overwhelming with its antiquity. It stood on a hill overlooking a beautiful village. Everyone in the village worked there in one capacity or other. The sun shone all the time—not like in

England where it is all too often too shy to come out from behind the clouds.'

'It was where you spent your childhood?'

'Most of it—although I did spend a great deal of time in my mother's house in England. My father was at his happiest when we returned to the chateau. *"This is where you want to be. This is where you are happiest,* ma petite—*where you belong,"* he always said to me. My mother was beautiful—made for happiness—and my father loved her dearly. She died giving birth to my brother—he died, too, without taking a breath. My father told me it happened sometimes. He was very sad after that, but happy that he had me.'

'And were you happy?'

'As happy as most people. People's contentment with life varies. My life was well ordered—inhibited—more so when my mother died. Happiness is rarely a permanent state—which ended for me when my aunt and uncle were killed.'

He looked at her steadily. 'One would be fortunate to achieve happiness all the time. And how are you now?' he asked, with a gentleness that touched Delphine. It was only a simple question, but there was so much sincerity in his voice that she looked at him with astonishment and studied him closely.

'I am as well as I can be—considering the unfortunate nature of my circumstances. Still, with time, I am sure the pain of losing my family will lessen,' she answered with a forced lightness.

Her grieving was evident to Laurence. Her expression became curiously soft, with a yearning quality that touched him. For a moment her face became unguarded and, for the first time in their short acquaintance, it showed him something of the lost child behind the deliberately maintained façade of the woman. His heart contracted at the grief he saw etched on her lovely face, and her amber eyes were so dark with suffering they were almost black. It was clear that losing her family so tragically had done a great deal of emotional damage.

'Your upbringing would have been very different from mine,' he remarked. 'The English are less formal than the French.'

'So many have been destroyed. I hate what has happened to France,' she said in a small voice, her expression subdued. 'It has become a cold, joyless place with no laughter.'

'And you like to laugh?'

'Yes, although my life has been wrapped in my work for so long I fear I might have forgotten how to.'

Laurence smiled, thinking her courageous and fresh and very lovely. With a ship's lantern shining on her, the colour on her face was gloriously high, which owed a great deal to the wind blowing the boat on. Her eyes were like sparkling orbs. They were the most brilliant eyes Laurence had ever seen, of an amber so bright they seemed lit from within. He was not a man of such iron control that he could resist looking down at her feminine form, which she held before him like a talisman.

Despite her youth she was no vapourish miss who would swoon at the first hurdle. Thinking of the pistols she had carried beneath her skirts, he held a deepening respect that she knew how to take care of herself. No doubt Sir Godfrey Bucklow had made sure she was trained in survival skills before sending her to France. When she looked at him with that forthright expression of confident determination, he knew he was right.

'You should laugh more often,' he murmured softly.

She sighed. 'I will, when I find something that amuses me. What will happen to France, do you think? You have been in Paris—have met the unfortunates in the Conciergerie.'

'Before I was arrested I saw much blood shed by the mob. I have had to ask myself where has the dignity, the self-control, the resolution gone in the France of today—a France that has killed its King and the Queen is a prisoner and likely to suffer the same fate. The people have their grievances—with some justification. It is only right and natural that they want change. The demands of the people should be listened to and acted on. Privilege must be abolished and all men should be taxed equally, according to their wealth.'

His companion tilted her head to one side and looked at him with interest. 'Anything else?'

'There are many others.'

'You speak like a politician. Perhaps that is something you should consider when you reach London.'

A cynical smile curved his lips. 'I don't think so.'

'Then what will you do?'

'Do I have to do anything?'

'I suspect you are not the sort of man who would be content to idle his days away doing nothing. You have to do something.'

'As to that, I shall have to decide what I am to do when I reach London.'

She regarded him intently. 'Are you a business-man?'

He grinned. Having no idea what his future might hold, he had no wish to commit himself to her questioning. 'You might say that—when I'm not spying for my country.'

'And is your business respectable?'

Her question made him smile. 'Perfectly respect-able,' he declared, enjoying being on the boat and beginning to wonder what life would be like as a smuggler. The very idea made him think of absolute freedom and appealed to his spirit of adventure. 'But if I were to tell you what I am thinking at this moment you might not agree. Besides, I do not wish to offend you but to quote your own words—*You know I am a British agent. That is all you need to know. All you want to know. It is best that way.*'

She scowled at him. 'I suppose I asked for that.'

He laughed. 'You did,' he said, sauntering away from her to speak to the skipper.

Delphine watched him go. Until she was seven-teen years old her life had been filled with joy. On that day when her beloved aunt and uncle went to the guillotine she had become concerned for the rights and miseries of others—also in the desperate hope that by doing so she would discover what had happened to her father.

She was not quite sure where she stood in society in relation to others, being half-French, half-English. Her father had seen to it that her life was divided equally between the two because it was what her mother would have wanted. In France she was treated as the daughter of Henri St Clair, Comte de la Clermont. In Cornwall she was allowed to roam free, to be herself without the restrictions imposed on her by her French relatives. It had been a blessing that when the troubles came to France, she was in England.

She stood at the rails, watching Guernsey draw nearer. The Englishman came to stand beside her.

'You look pensive. What are you thinking of?'

'Oh, nothing in particular.' She smiled. 'And you? You will be taken to London. I imagine you will be very busy. There will be so much to catch up with.'

He nodded. 'Yes, I imagine there will be.' He looked at her. 'I will not forget you. I appreciate what you have done for me. Without you I would still be rotting in the Conciergerie—or worse.'

'No, you wouldn't. Someone else would have been given the task of getting you out.'

'The circumstances of our time together have been unfortunate. At any other time I would like to have got to know you better.'

'Who knows what the future holds for either of us?' she said quietly. 'We may even meet again—if we continue in our line of work. We'll soon be arriving on Guernsey. It's where we will part company.'

He turned to face her. 'I have enjoyed knowing you, Sophie—or whatever it is you are called.'

'It has been interesting. When you are back in England you will forget all about this.'

'That statement is completely false. I think you know that.'

'I am honoured, but you, Citizen Blanchard, flatter us both.'

'It is quite natural after what you have done for me. You are different from anyone I have ever met.'

She smiled. 'No two people are the same.'

'No, but most people I have met arouse little interest in me. You are different. I think I would find it interesting to discover more.'

'I think we know each other well enough. You will soon be on your way to London.'

'And you? Will you be going to London?'

'No.'

'So you think to escape me.'

'You make me sound like your prisoner.'

His gaze was warm as he looked down at her. 'Heaven forbid I would do that to you. It is the reverse. It is I who am yours.'

She laughed. 'Now you truly are jesting. I am not the kind of woman to be bowled over by a handsome face and a winsome smile, so you are wasting your time if you are looking for an easy conquest.'

'I don't believe you are. You know how to wound a man.'

'I believe in being frank.'

'Which I always admire in anyone. But I think you misunderstand me.'

'I understand you very well. We have been thrown together by circumstance. Do not attach more significance to it than that.'

He took her hands and drew her towards him. He was very close. She was not small, but he was some six or seven inches taller, and she had to look up at him. She was eager to let him know that she was not affected by his proximity.

'It has been more than that.'

Delphine thought that in that moment he was going to kiss her and she felt alarmed, particularly as she realised that it was not so much him she was afraid of, but herself. Impatiently she tried to shake off the impression he was having on her. Why had she allowed herself to be attracted by him? Why was she hoping that he would kiss her and yet at the same time she was hoping he wouldn't? Perhaps she had been alone with him too long.

He took her hands and, raising them, placed a kiss lightly on the back of her fingers. She tried not to show surprise or emotion. When he released them she turned and looked at the surroundings as *The Seagull* sailed into the harbour.

With the coastal cliffs and castle, a harbour fortification in St Peter Port, it was a perfect place for smugglers. Lobster pots were stacked around the harbour along with nets drying on poles, and boats secured to their moorings, and the crew of vessels and fishermen milling about. There was a strong smell of fish on the air. They tied up at the quayside and left the boat.

She saw three men walking towards the boat, recognising one of them as being Sir Godfrey Bucklow. His hair was fine and white and he was tall and lean, holding himself extremely erect for all his sixty years, which had much to do with his time as a soldier. He was an influential and wealthy man who lived in the north of Cornwall, where he owned an estate and several properties. He also held a position of importance at the Foreign Office in London.

'See,' Delphine said to the Englishman. 'There is Sir Godfrey come to meet me with two other gentlemen—your reception committee, I expect.'

Seeing another boat which was familiar to her and recognising the skipper as being from Fowey, she stopped and had a word with him before giving her attention to Sir Godfrey. He had come to the island to meet her along with the two other serious-faced gentlemen. They had been on the island for several days, awaiting the expected arrival of the Englishman. After introductions were made and congratulations on a successful mission, Delphine stepped away with Sir Godfrey and watched as the three men walked away.

Chapter Four

'The Englishman must indeed be an important personage to warrant two gentlemen making the journey to Guernsey to meet him,' Delphine murmured.

'He is,' Sir Godfrey answered. 'Come. You have done well, Delphine. I confess that I had my doubts, but you were determined to take on the task. You look tired. When do you expect to leave the island?'

She looked towards a boat. 'Tomorrow night. The skipper of the vessel that is to take me to Cornwall won't be ready to leave until then—providing the conditions are favourable. I was hoping to leave before then.'

'I imagine you were. I took the liberty of reserving a room for you at the inn I'm staying at.'

'Thank you. I appreciate that.'

They walked on, following in the wake of the others. The ground rose quite steeply from the dockside and, climbing a steep flight of stone steps running between tall houses, they reached the inn where they were all to stay the night.

'Do you know the skipper of the boat that will take you to Cornwall, Delphine?'

'Why?' she asked. 'Please don't tell me that after braving the mobs of Paris and helping a prisoner escape from the Conciergerie, you are concerned that I will come to grief in a local fishing boat,' she said teasingly.

His grey eyes were shrewd and steady and had lost none of their youthful sparkle. 'You cannot blame me for being concerned—and not for one minute do I believe that boat is used for fishing. I have no doubt it's packed with cargo of a different kind.'

She laughed. 'I don't doubt it—and I'm touched by your concern for my safety. Rest assured that I do know the skipper—he makes regular trips to Guernsey and will take me to Fowey.'

'Aye, well, he'll have to have his wits about him if he hopes to dodge the Revenue Cutters. The Royal Navy is also making its presence known since war broke out between Britain and France. I'll be returning to London tomorrow with the two gentlemen who are eager to hear what the Englishman has to say, but I wanted to be here to make sure you arrived safely. We are grateful for all you have done, Delphine, but you know the dangers. What if something should happen to you? Have you not thought what an impact it would have on your grandfather?'

'I know full well the risks I take. If anything should happen to me I know you would tell him— and my aunt.'

'Then it is fortunate the two of them don't speak

otherwise you would have no alibi for your absences.'
He glanced at her as she continued to watch the English-
glishman disappear into the night. 'This Englishman.
He has made an impression on you.'

'As you see, I have survived the encounter without
coming to grief. He is an impressive person.'

'Don't you think it's about time you told your
grandfather what it is that you do, Delphine?'

'No. I cannot. I want it to remain that way. I know
his thoughts on the subject. If I am so intent on helping those trying to get out of France he would say my
ambition would be better served with a suitable husband. But his health is failing, Sir Godfrey.'

'I know this isn't what you want to hear, but there
may be some sense in that.'

'What? A husband?' She sighed, shaking her head.
'I don't know. Could I relinquish what I do for marriage? I know I cannot carry on doing what I do in-
definitely. It will have to come to an end sooner or
later, I know that—I may never return to France. But
marriage?'

It was a subject Delphine had given thought to
often, but with an uncertain future looming ahead
of her she had refused to look it squarely in the eye.
She would not marry just anyone. There would be
no inept youth with groping hands and wet kisses
for her, but a man, someone to love her with all the
masculine authority at his command—experienced,
bold and dashing—like Citizen Claude Blanchard,
perhaps, or whoever he was. She was shocked and
instantly ashamed of the way her mind was working.

The Englishman was totally unsuitable in every way and it was a ridiculous thought which she dismissed at once—but she could not deny it.

'And your grandfather's failing health?' Sir Godfrey said, interrupting her thoughts.

'I know. I think I should stay and take care of him.'

He nodded. 'That is as it should be. I will not contact you for a while. No news of your father?'

She shook her head. 'No, but I won't give up on him. You will continue to make enquiries on my behalf? Someone might know something.'

'I will.'

Chapter Five

The day was warm. From the window of the inn where Delphine had spent the night, luxuriating in a bath and a change of clothes, she could see the port was busy with vessels loading and unloading cargo and carting it to and from the warehouses close to the quay.

After a while, with nothing else to do with her day other than wait for the boat to take her to Cornwall, attired in a plain blue gown with white lace bordering the bodice, she set off to walk away from the port.

'Sophie,' a voice said behind her and something inside her crumbled at the sound of her name in the Englishman's mouth. Running her tongue over her lips, she swallowed the dryness in her throat before turning. His face held an expression that Delphine could not identify and made her heart clench in her chest. She wanted to look away, but she couldn't.

'Oh—I didn't expect to see you. I thought you

would be fully occupied with the gentlemen who arrived with Sir Godfrey.'

'We'll all be leaving later today. And you?'

'I have friends on Guernsey. I will remain a while.'

He cocked a quizzical dark brow and a knowing smile played on his lips. 'I saw you conversing with the skipper of one of the boats in the harbour earlier. He is a friend of yours?'

'I know several people on the island. The skipper you saw me speaking to is a fisherman by trade.'

'Fishermen?' He gave her a dubious stare. 'And you're sure about that, are you?'

She laughed. 'Well—in their spare time they fish—and at other times...'

'They sail to Guernsey to take advantage of the tax-free goods to sell on in England.'

'Something like that.'

A pair of seagulls let out raucous cries as they did battle over a dead fish, but Delphine was deaf to them. It was as if they receded into a mist, while she and the Englishman were isolated in a pool of sunlight where every sense was intensified. He had changed his clothes and looked incredibly handsome in a blue frock coat and a froth of lace at his throat, the whiteness of it emphasising the darkness of his hair drawn back in a queue.

'Where are you going?'

'For a walk,' she replied. 'I have to do something with my day and after being cooped up in the chaise for such a long period, the idea of stretching my legs was too tempting to resist.'

'Then do you mind if I accompany you? I, too, have a little time to kill.'

'By all means.'

'Are you hungry?' he asked, seeing a pie seller and smelling the delicious aroma of cooked pies.

'It's been a while since breakfast—and, yes, I am hungry.'

'Then I will buy us both a pie.'

'Fresh from the oven they are,' the pie seller said, seeing them approach. 'Baked by my wife's own fair hands.' He waited for them to choose and passed the food over.

Finding a wall to sit on overlooking the harbour, they proceeded to eat the pies, so hot they had to juggle them between their fingers. Neither of them spoke until they had finished eating.

'That was so good,' Delphine said, licking her fingers and brushing the crumbs from her skirt, shooing away the gulls that had gathered hoping for a tasty morsel.

Taking out a handkerchief, Claude wiped his hands and smiled when he saw a dribble of gravy on her chin. 'Allow me,' he said, gently brushing the gravy away, his smile creasing his eyes. 'Shall we walk on?'

Finding herself close to and being stared at by this magnetic, thoroughly compelling man with that confident gaze made her heart beat faster. Stepping back, she looked away. 'It's a relief not to have to hide away,' she said as they walked to a quiet place on the shore. With the sun shining on the water, everything looked so still and sleepy. 'You will soon be back in

London—so very different from all this. I like being close to the sea, to feel the salt spray stinging my cheeks and the sound of the waves against the shore.'

'I agree with you. I haven't done anything like this for a long time—strolling along a shore with a pretty girl.' He spoke quietly, watching her. 'I know I've said this before, but I really am going to miss you.'

As she met his gaze, the air rang with the truth of it. She looked into his bright green eyes and let anticipation flutter in her belly. 'You'll soon forget all about me when you get home.'

'No, I won't. You are not the kind of person one can forget.' He stopped walking and, reaching out his hand, tilted her face to his. 'How could I forget you? I have never met a woman like you—how you are prepared to put your life in danger for others. You are quite extraordinary.'

'I told you my father is missing. I want to know what happened to him—where he is—if he's still alive—which is why I go to France, hoping someone will have seen him—somewhere.'

'Will you go back?'

'Some time, perhaps.' Glancing back the way they had come, she hadn't realised they had walked so far. They were close to the sea, sheltered by rocks, away from curious eyes. 'I'd best be getting back. Sir Godfrey will be leaving with you.'

He moved to stand close to her. Aware of his nearness, Delphine turned her head, her breath soft and fragrant as she looked into his eyes. Her hands grew cold with sweat and her legs began to tremble. Something was happening between them and she wasn't sure what it was, only that it was something strange to her, something that had never happened to her before.

'Dear Lord, Sophie,' he whispered. 'Leaving you—this is going to be harder than I realised…' Her mind reeled as he pulled her slowly towards him. She went easily, each step unimpeded, until she leaned against him. She felt the strength of his arms and the warmth of his masculine body. She told herself that this should not be happening, but she did nothing to pull away from him. She could feel the hard muscles of his broad chest and smell his maleness. A tautness began in her breast, a delicious ache that was like a languorous, honeyed warmth. She turned her face up to his and he brushed the hair back from her face, his fingers infinitely gentle.

It seemed a lifetime passed as they gazed at each other. In that lifetime each lived through a range of deep, tender emotions new to them both, exquisite emotions that neither of them could put into words. As though in slow motion, unable to resist the temptation her mouth offered, slowly the Englishman's own moved inexorably closer. His gaze was gentle and compelling when, in a sweet, mesmeric sensation, his mouth found hers. Delphine melted into him and yielded her mouth with a long sobbing moan. The kiss was long and lingeringly slow.

Raising his head, Laurence gazed down at her in wonder. 'My God!' he whispered, his voice hoarse. 'You are so sweet.'

Her lips quirked in a little smile. 'I have been called many things, but never sweet.'

'And you do like me?'

'Yes, I like you.'

'Then another kiss I would have—to confirm what your lips have just told me,' Claude murmured.

Closing her eyes, she yielded to him, pressing herself against his body. A strange, alien feeling fluttered within her breast and she was halted for a brief passage of time when she found her lips entrapped with his once more and, though they were soft and tender, they burned with a fire that scorched her.

Their bodies strained together hungrily in a mindless rapture while the gulls screeched overhead. Never having known anything like she felt at that moment, never having felt anything that was so disabling to her senses, she melted under his fierce, fevered kiss.

She clung to him as she gave herself wholly to his passion, becoming so enmeshed in its intensity that she found herself returning it with a wild and free abandon that amazed her as well as him. She felt his arms go round her, hold her close to his chest and her heart streamed into his. She had no strength to pit against his will and her own need, yet as his hand brushed her breast she twisted from him wildly.

'Please—we must not do this. I cannot.'

Claude looked down at her, while his breathing slowed in time and he said very low, 'I want you. I have tried to fight it all the time we have been together, and I cannot pretend otherwise. There is no need for us to part. Come with me, Sophie. Come with me to London.'

He spoke softly, his voice so piercingly sweet it sounded to her that the meaning of his words came slowly. She could hardly think what to do, with her head spinning after that thrilling brush with passion—but London? How could she do that—and in what capacity did he want her to go with him? As his mistress—his wife? Although, when she recalled their conversation in the woods and he had agreed with her with clinical calm of what his idea of a wife should be, she very much doubted he would propose marriage to her. Besides, she would not marry anyone who harboured such views and she would most certainly not be his mistress.

'What are you saying—that I become your mistress?'

'I will be honest with you, Sophie. I have no idea what awaits me in London, but if you were there—if we were together—we could certainly get to know each other better. Surely we can snatch a little happiness, a little joy from life. We are compatible, after all.'

Mortified and humiliated almost beyond bearing, Delphine could not believe what she was hearing. There was an aura of calm authority about him. His expression was now blank and impervious and he looked unbearably handsome. The sight of his chiselled features and bold green eyes never failed to stir her heart. But events seemed to be whirling beyond her control.

Reaching out, he drew her to him once more, but

she placed her hands firmly against his chest and pushed him away. Raising her head, she met his gaze.

'I don't think I like your proposal,' she told him, wanting to conceal how deeply hurt, angry and insulted she was after what had just happened between them. 'I am not easily persuaded—not even when you kiss me so passionately. You have caught me unawares—in a moment of weakness. It must be the heat, or the fact—the relief—that we are safe. But whatever it is, this must end now. I cannot allow you to distract me from my purpose.'

'I will not do that. I agree. I did not mean this to happen, but it has. There will be no repeat of this—unless you wish it.'

'No, I most certainly do not. If I were to do that, I would despise myself.'

'And despise me?' He spoke low and gentle.

She looked at him with pain-filled eyes. 'No. I could never despise you, but what you are suggesting does not endear you to me in the least. Do not torture me like this. It is unworthy of you.'

'That is not my intention. You would get used to the idea. London is an exciting place. Come with me. Board the vessel with me when it sails. It's not a difficult decision.'

Delphine stared at him incredulously, almost speechless with rage. He was smiling that half-smile that had been attractive to her before, but now infuriated her. Now she longed to slap his arrogant, insufferable face. 'Difficult? You told me that you admired me, admired what I do, then, after all I have done to secure your freedom, you make that despicable offer that I become your mistress.

'How can you do that—to ask me to put myself and my virtue at your disposal. I know exactly what I would be—a diversion—one of those women who fill a need until you find yourself a wife with the right pedigree and wealth, a woman who will run your household as she has been taught to do.' Drawing a deep breath, her fists clenched, she glared at him. 'You beast. You are the most conceited, self-centred, egotistical man I have ever had the misfortune to meet and the sooner we part company the better.'

His eyes narrowed and his face darkened. 'Who are you really, Sophie Blanchard?'

Stepping back, she looked at him coldly. The face of her father came into her mind—her father, proud, splendid and sad—and then the face of her grandfather, equally as proud as her father. With that the desperately loving Delphine shrank away from this man who would destroy her and sully her good name of Delphine St Clair.

Shaking her head slowly, she stepped away from him. A deadly calm settled over her, banishing everything but her hurt and disappointment. Her small chin lifted, her spine stiffened as she put up a valiant effort for control—a fight she won. She stood before him looking like a proud young queen, her eyes sparking like twin jewels.

'It doesn't matter now. Better you don't know. Not knowing will make it easier for you to forget me—and your insulting offer that I become your mistress—without any feeling or emotion. Please don't think that because you kissed me you have to make some kind of commitment.'

'Life isn't like that. I have kissed many women I have been attracted to, but that doesn't mean to say that I had to commit myself to them.'

Delphine was conscious of a sudden surge to her anger, realising just how stupid and naive she had been. How dare he treat what had just happened between them casually, as if the kiss was insignificant and meant nothing out of the ordinary and he was used to kissing ladies all over the place. 'I do not have your experience. Apart from yourself, no other man has kissed me,' she told him, giving him an insight into just how truly innocent she was.

'I'm sorry you feel that way. There's no reason why we can't enjoy ourselves. I am not prepared to pledge eternal vows—'

'I wouldn't expect you to do that,' she fumed. 'I certainly don't have the right credentials to be your wife—only an ancient pedigree that was taken from me by the revolution. A fortune is something I don't have.'

'That doesn't matter. I find you an adorable, enchanting creature. I don't offer you solemn love or soulful devotion. I offer you my protection, affection and fun.'

His voice was like pure silk and his eyes became warm and appreciative, but when Delphine thought of what he was asking of her she felt fury explode in her, not just with him and the effrontery of what he wanted, but at the sudden excitement that stirred in her at the very idea. Never had she been so humiliated in her life, she told herself, whipping up her temper until her cheeks were scarlet with outrage.

'I don't think I would like your kind of fun. You are asking me to dishonour myself. The proposition is unacceptable to me. I have too much regard and self-respect for myself to become any man's mistress. My father is a good man. He taught me right from wrong. When I give myself to a man it will be within the bounds of marriage—not some tainted liaison with a libertine. I am worth more than that. You do not deserve that I should abase myself for you.

'What I do now—my work in France—is honest work. Decent work. Nothing tawdry or shameful, which is what I would be were I to become your plaything—your whore. Since I have not the slightest intention of going with you to London, in whatever capacity you intend, I think we should end this conversation since it is going nowhere.'

Her words hit Laurence like a douche of cold water. They hung in the air between them, bringing Laurence to his senses, and he stared at her anew. His conscience, which he had assumed was long since dead, chose that moment to resurrect itself. Expelling a ragged breath and out of sheer self-preservation, he stepped away from her, raking fingers of angry self-disgust and disappointment through his hair as he fought to reassemble his senses and bring his desire under control.

Each day her hold upon his very thoughts had grown stronger. He had not felt such attraction for a woman in a long time and never as strong as this, but he must fight it, which he repeated to himself for good measure. They were to go their separate ways and, until he knew what awaited him, he could not allow himself to become distracted.

He realised how little he knew about Sophie. She had told him of her French background, but who was she now? He didn't even know her real name. Was she a member of the nobility? But then, if so, how could a woman constrained by society do what she did? Like a siren in Greek mythology whose singing was believed to lure sailors to destruction on the rocks, her very nearness had lured him to her, and her sudden vulnerability that he had felt when he had held her in his arms had finally broken all bounds of his restraint. He drew back sharply.

'You are right. I apologise if I have offended you and for allowing my ardour to get the better of me. We both need to be focused on what we are about to do.'

Delphine had walked away from him, leaving him standing on the shore. She didn't go down to the quay to see them off on the vessel that would take them to London. Having boarded the boat that was to take her home, she looked wistfully back towards Guernsey, the wind blowing her hair about her face. The lights from the buildings glittered yellow in the dark and then, as the island receded further away into the darkness like something seen in a dream, they disappeared altogether. The wake of the boat foamed whitely in the moonlight.

The skipper of the vessel and some of the crew, who were well-organised smugglers, were familiar to her. Their main sources of danger were the Royal Navy and the Revenue Cutters, but a fast lugger like the one she was on could outrun them and the skipper felt it was safe to make the crossing to Cornwall. She stood at the rails for a long time, knowing that the coast of Cornwall was coming closer.

With the sea all around her, she felt nothing inside but a well of emptiness and a profound loneliness that stretched before her like a never-ending road. Anguish was something she was accustomed to in her life and now it washed over her like a tidal wave. She felt a tightening of her throat and a chill about her body that had nothing to do with the wind blowing the vessel onwards.

She thought of the Englishman, not quite understanding why she felt such a connection between them, a connection that had been there before their kiss. It was a bond of some sort, improbable as that might seem—the kiss had proved that. She was excited by him. He made her feel a sense of adventure, but he'd had to go and spoil it. Recalling the moment when she had brought him out of the Conciergerie, her initial opinion had been that he was an arrogant nobleman, a rake, playing at being a spy. He had proved her right by proposing that she become his mistress and she could not forgive him for that.

* * *

The wind held and the boat made good time, arriving in Fowey harbour when dawn was breaking. After Delphine was rowed to the shore, the boat would sail west to a safe haven where the cargo would be unloaded. As she stepped on to English soil, Delphine felt her desire to return to France gradually slipping away from her. Here were two remaining members of her mother's family, her grandfather and his sister, her Great-Aunt Amelia.

Aunt Amelia had married young, but her husband, a naval man, was killed at sea not long after their marriage. It was before Delphine's time but, according to Agatha, her grandfather's housekeeper, at fifty years old Aunt Amelia had fallen in love with Sir Richard Plomley, a married man and the owner of the Pendene estate adjoining her grandfather's land. The two would not be parted. At the time her aunt lived in a rented house in Fowey, a house she lived in to this day.

Her grandfather had been wild with fury at what he saw as his sister's disloyalty and wanton behaviour. For her to disgrace their family name in this way was more than he could bear. The fondness they had once had for each other had ended when Aunt Amelia had refused to end the affair and their affection for each other had frozen over with the bitter enmity that had come between them. They had not spoken to each other since.

Delphine made her way into the town, arriving at the row of elegant houses where her Great-Aunt Amelia lived. Delphine had taken on several missions to help people escape from France and had been glad when the mission was complete and she could return to her grandfather—he none the wiser, always surmising she was with her great-aunt in Fowey.

Being so early and knowing her aunt would be abed for a couple of hours yet, and having no wish to disturb her, she collected her horse from the stable behind the house and, hatless and astride, her long legs gripping her mount, her hair blowing loose in the wind, she was soon galloping home.

She approached the sturdy door of Tregannon House, the stone Cornish house that had been in her mother's family for nigh on two hundred years. Aged to different shades of grey, it was a large two-storey house with windows that overlooked the sea. Ivy climbed up the walls and the chimney. Only a ten-acre tract of land remained of the original three hundred that had been sold off gradually over the decades.

The house when Delphine entered it wrapped itself around her like a comforting blanket. She had come to love the old place over the years and, now she no longer had the chateau to go to in France, she looked on it as her home. She found her grandfather eating his breakfast in the dining room, Agatha, the ageing housekeeper and only servant at Tregannon, hovering over the table holding a coffee pot. Her face broke into smiles when she saw Delphine.

'So here you are—and as welcome as the flowers

in May. How was your aunt when you left her?' Agatha asked, proceeding to pour Delphine a cup of the aromatic beverage.

'She—she was as she always is—quite well,' Delphine uttered, pulling out a chair and sitting across from her grandfather. 'How are you, Grandfather? Have you missed me?'

'The house has been peaceful,' he muttered, stabbing a piece of bacon and shoving it into his mouth.

'Really, Grandfather, I'm as quiet as a mouse as well you know,' she retorted, laughing lightly and taking a welcome sip of her coffee.

'I'll go and get you some breakfast,' Agatha said, going to the door. 'You'll be needing something after riding all the way from Fowey.'

'Thank you, Agatha. I'm starving.' She looked at her grandfather bent forward and hunched over his breakfast. His distinguishing features were his bushy white eyebrows above deep-set eyes and a thick white sweep of hair from his broad brow. There was a strong thrust to his jaw and his youth was lost in the gathering furrows of age.

When Agatha brought her breakfast she ate ravenously, not having eaten since leaving Guernsey.

Her grandfather cleared his throat thunderously, giving her a piercing look. 'Was there any message for me from Amelia?'

'No, Grandfather, and nor would there be when you keep each other at arm's length. Neither of you is getting any younger and to carry on this—this feud like this is quite ridiculous. You really should bury your pride and go and see her—or invite her to Tregannon.'

'Hmm,' he grumbled. 'She knows where I live.'

Delphine sighed. It was an argument they'd often had with no result. Delphine had tried bringing them together many times, but to no avail. In fact, she really believed they took a certain malicious pleasure in annoying each other. The window of the dining room overlooked the garden, and there Agatha's husband, Cecil, was busy with a wheelbarrow. He kept the garden immaculate, which could be said of Agatha and the way she kept the house. Everything was kept in order. The furniture and the wooden floors gleamed and the smell of beeswax filled every room.

Her grandfather laid down his napkin and stared at her as she tucked into ham and eggs and warm bread and butter. 'You're late,' he said. 'I didn't expect you to stay with Amelia longer than a couple of days. I suppose gallivanting about Fowey and riding hither and thither is more important to you than marriage. You are twenty-one. It's high time you thought of settling down, Delphine. Your mother had been married three years before she reached that age. I owe it to both your parents to see you wed before my demise.'

Delphine had made it a point not to argue with her grandfather, although acquiescing gnawed at her. She tapped her foot impatiently under the table. Words clamoured to be spoken. It was hard not to tell him how she felt, but, concerned about what would happen to her when he was gone, she knew how badly he wanted her wed.

'Mother was fortunate. She would have been hard-pressed to find a more considerate and kinder man than my father. Find me a man as fine as he is and I will marry him tomorrow.'

'You cannot blame me for wanting to see you settled—the future after I'm gone is uncertain.'

'And you think marriage is best for my future.'

'I do. If you continue as you do, then you will find yourself an old maid.'

'Better that than to be saddled for a lifetime with a man I have no liking for.' Tilting her head to one side, she looked across at him. 'If I didn't know how much you care for me, Grandfather, I would think you are trying to get rid of me.' Without giving him time to answer she got to her feet, walking round the table and planting a kiss on the top of his head. 'I'll take my leave of you now. I'm going for a bath. It was a long ride from Fowey and I smell of horses.'

She was halfway across the room when his voice halted her. 'Consider my words, Delphine. Would you deny a dying man?'

On a sigh she turned and looked at him. 'Grandfather, that's not fair. You use that fact to bend me to your will—to try to frighten me.'

'Good. Then we do not need to cross swords any longer.'

She smiled, an engaging, wonderful smile that would have brought any other man to his knees in admiration of her beauty. 'I think we do, Grandfather. You enjoy the verbal fencing as much as I.'

'So now we will dispense with the play on words

and have some honesty between us. According to Dr Harris I haven't much time left. However, this is not important. What is important is your future. You are still my beloved granddaughter and I want to see you happy. Now go and get your bath and we will speak of it later.'

Leaving the room, Delphine felt tears spring into her eyes and it was with an effort that she held them back. These arguments with her grandfather happened all too frequently of late and she always schooled herself carefully to present a cool, insouciant exterior, having resolved long ago that she would not be browbeaten into marriage. But she knew her grandfather had reason on his side and she had the sense to know that the time would come when her heart and mind would have to bend before necessity and it would be sooner rather than later.

When she was alone she felt the weight of her misery. In a short time, if her grandfather had his way, she would be married to a complete stranger, to lose the independence she had acquired over the past two years. It was true that she was free to choose for herself, but there was no one.

Chapter Six

Eight weeks after returning to England, for the first time since he was a boy Laurence came to Pendene. He climbed out of the carriage and let his gaze skim the house and surrounding grounds with a critical eye. It wasn't how he'd imagined it to be. The Pendene estate had been in his mother's family for close on three hundred years—save during the Commonwealth years. He remembered it as being a fine house. It had changed as he had changed. They were both in need of loving care.

On his return to London, on a visit to his lawyer he discovered that things were worse than he had imagined. Because of the enormous debts left by his father, his own private income was gone. His mother's legacy was gone—all vanished into nothing. He thanked God his sisters had both married well and he didn't have them to take care of. Shame and despair, and the feeling that his own father had betrayed him, felled him.

He had two assets to his name. The London house

and a rundown estate with a defunct copper mine in Cornwall. One had to go. Before he made up his mind which, he'd decided to take a look at Pendene. Now, as he looked around, he smiled when he recalled how happy he'd been here playing with his two sisters under the watchful eye of their mother—riding their ponies, running through the woods and learning to swim in the sea. Those were the memories he treasured—and there were other, more recent, memories he now treasured, memories of a girl with warm amber eyes and golden hair and lips more soft and tempting than any he had known.

When he had parted from Sophie on Guernsey he had felt a loss that was beyond anything he had ever felt in his life. Despite his belief to the contrary, when he had arrived in London he had found it no easy matter thrusting her out of his mind. He threw himself into sorting out matters concerning the house and other issues that had cropped up during his long absence, but it was Sophie he saw in his mind, Sophie who stole his thoughts away from important matters at hand.

He tortured himself by thinking of the way she had refused to become his mistress and how cruelly he had mocked her. He dragged his thoughts from the torment of that time. He preferred the more refined torture of thinking about the joy of her, their light banter on their journey to Granville. He thought of the way she had melted against him and kissed him with innocent passion, how warm she had felt in his arms, wonderful and loving. Her face came to him again and again. Soft and resolute, her flesh pale and translucent, with sharply angled brows and high cheekbones and soft amber eyes. It was an arresting face, riveting, the sort of face you saw across a crowded ballroom and never forgot.

Where was she? Who was she? What was she doing now?

Cursing himself for behaving like a love-smitten youth, he tried to divert his irrational thoughts away from her, but it became an internal battle—one he began to lose a little more with each passing day. He'd even gone as far as to seek out Sir Godfrey Bucklow at his club to ask him to give him her identity, only to be thwarted when informed that Sir Godfrey was out of town and was unlikely to return soon.

Now as he walked around Pendene, inspecting every aspect of it, he asked himself if he could sell it. Or could he uproot himself and live in Cornwall, leave behind the pleasures to be had in London and his work with the Intelligence Service, even though his superiors were pressing him to continue? There was a living to be made on the estate, but a poor one, and its biggest drawback was that it was landlocked. But as he ventured off his land on to that of his neighbour and made his way to the cove and looked out to sea, his mind began churning.

The land was poor, with gorse growing on it and only fit for sheep, but poor as it was Laurence wanted it. 'Who does this land belong to?' he enquired of John McGuire. John had managed the estate for years, dividing his time between Pendene and his first love, the sea. But he did not neglect estate duties.

'Jacob Arlington over at Tregannon.'

'Would he sell it, do you think?'

'He might, for the right price. He's old and in poor health—although I have to say there's more than one landowner interested in this tract, the cove being the attraction. There's—also something I think you should know before you see him.'

'Oh? And what might that be?'

'A scandal that may determine whether the old man feels inclined to sell the land to you or not.'

'Then I shall have to try to persuade him. You'd better tell me, John.'

When John had left him, having recounted to him the whole sorry saga of how his uncle had openly conducted an affair with Jacob Arlington's sister while his wife was ailing, Laurence was not dissuaded. Nothing ventured, nothing gained was his motto.

Standing on the cliff looking down at the cove, he could not believe the turn of events. His mood was restless. Here was a new future. His uncle had closed the mine when it began to show lower and lower profits and he'd had no wish to sink more capital into it. Laurence's lawyer, after contacting the Plomleys' family lawyer in St Austell for details concerning the estate, had given him an estimate of the likely cost of reopening the mine. He'd made enquiries on Laurence's behalf and he was happy to report that it was far from exhausted and had potential.

That was the moment Laurence made his decision.

He would sell the house in London and use some of the proceeds to reopen the mine and buy the land—if Jacob Arlington could be persuaded to sell it to him—and perhaps a boat. Suddenly it was important to him that he had a boat.

As he rode to Tregannon with more confidence than when he'd arrived at Pendene, his spirit of adventure had returned and was riding high. Whatever Jacob Arlington was asking for the tract of land he would pay it—but he was to discover the purchase held a clause, one he could not ignore.

Unbeknown to Laurence, the matter of Jacob Arlington's granddaughter's future was resolved sooner than he could have hoped when Laurence arrived at the house. He was received in the drawing room.

'Welcome to Tregannon, Lord Beaumont. It's many years since a member of your family came here.'

Laurence nodded. 'I am here to introduce myself. I am not unaware of the circumstances that came between our families some years back. But that was then. Things change. I thank you for seeing me.'

'You are welcome, Lord Beaumont—and you are right. What happened is in the past, an unsavoury business, but I will not allow it to dictate the future. Are you to take up permanent residence at Pendene?'

'That is my intention—although the place has been neglected for a long time and there is much to be done.'

They sat and talked of local matters and under the old man's close scrutiny and piercing gaze, Laurence told him of his intention to reopen the mine.

'Then I wish you well with that. It would certainly be welcome to the people hereabouts. Many are without work and families go hungry. I know it wasn't worked out when it shut down—but you will need people to advise you.'

'I realise that. However, it is not the mine that has brought me to see you. There is another matter I wish to discuss with you.'

Jacob smiled thinly. 'And would I be correct in thinking that this matter concerns a certain parcel of land?'

Laurence gave him a sombre look. 'It does. I would like to buy it—if it's for sale.'

'It might be—for the right price.'

'And what would that be?'

'I expect it to be a rather lengthy discussion. I'll have refreshment sent in.'

Not until Agatha had brought them some tea did they continue with the discussion.

'Tell me, Lord Beaumont, are you married by any chance?'

'No, I am not. I've had little time to give to settling down. I worked for British Intelligence—for the past twelve months I've been a prisoner in the Conciergerie in Paris, fully expecting the powers that be to execute me at any time. Fortunately I was one of the lucky ones who managed to escape. Now I'm back in England I'm anxious to tread a different path, so to speak, and make my life here—in Cornwall.'

'And your work with the Intelligence Service?'

'I'm finished with that. So, about the land?'

'Yes—of course. I will sell you the land, Lord Beaumont—but a proviso comes with it which you may not like.'

Laurence raised his eyebrows. 'A proviso. Tell me.'

When Jacob told him he would sell him the land with the proviso that he married his granddaughter, Delphine, after he got over the initial shock, Laurence left to think it over, but in his mind's eye all he could see was a girl with warm amber eyes and golden hair.

After riding to Fowey to visit her aunt, Delphine arrived back at Tregannon to see a horse and rider disappearing down the drive.

'You've had a visitor, Grandfather,' she said when she joined him in his study.

'Yes—and a surprise it was.'

'Who was it?'

'The man I have chosen for you to marry,' he told her—he never had been one to beat about the bush when something needed saying.

She stared at him. 'But—you can't.'

'I can and I have. I repeat, Delphine—before my demise I want to see you settled.'

'To speak with such certainty, you must think the gentleman is suitable.'

'I do and I do not believe he will give you cause for reproach. He will have no wish to constrain you and you will not lose the freedom you hold so dear. If there was a man you loved, a man who loved you enough to marry you and be worthy of the name you bear, then I should not oppose it. As things stand at this time there is no one, so I have chosen one for you.'

He spoke in such decisive tones that for a moment Delphine could find nothing to say. She could only stammer helplessly, 'But…but if I do not like this man and do not wish to marry him? What then? I am of an age to choose my own husband.'

'That is true, but you know I love you and I ask you to trust me.'

Her grandfather had the grace to pause when he spoke so harshly, so pointedly, and Delphine knew he regretted the strength of his words. But his blood was up and there was no stopping him.

'Perhaps it is wrong of me, but it is only my great love for you and my selfishness that I would live a long life that has kept me from finding you a husband before. But I can put it off no longer.'

'How? How did you find him?'

'I didn't. He found me. His uncle was Sir Richard Plomley and he's taking up residence in Pendene. He came earlier to ask if I would sell him the strip of land.'

'What is his name, Grandfather? Who is he?'

'Lord Beaumont—a man who until recently was connected to the Foreign Office.'

'And did you agree to sell the land to him?'

'Yes—on one proviso.'

'And what was that?'

'That he takes you into the bargain.'

Delphine stared at him. Never in her life had she felt so shocked, so humiliated. 'And what did he say?'

'He's gone away to think about it. There is no longer anything for you in France—that disappeared when the revolution came along, along with members of your French family. If I waited for you to choose, you'd end up alone. I'm not going to let that happen to you. Your mother would haunt me to the end of my days—and I haven't many of them left—if I were to leave you a spinster.

'I know you will be angry with me, but that can't be helped. I also know you believe your father is still alive, but I doubt it and you will have to face that fact. There is no inheritance here—nothing but debts and a crumbling pile of stones. The rest of the land is gone—solely to pay the debts. The only piece left is the ten acres which includes the cove.'

'Which Lord Beaumont wants to buy.'

'Aye—and every Plomley before him.'

'And if he refuses to take me as part of the deal?'

'Then I will sell the land to someone else. He's not the only one who wants it—and let's face it, with access to the cove, it would prove advantageous to the smugglers up and down the coast. But he's a single man—a good man—a handsome devil, too, which should appeal to you,' he went on, sensing his advantage. 'If he offers you marriage, you should grasp it with both hands. It is an inestimable offer.'

'For whom?' Delphine uttered tightly. 'I see nothing of value in it. I suspect he doesn't want to marry me any more than I him.'

'He will.'

'But what about the old scandal, Grandfather? How

can you even consider a union between me and a member of that family after what happened between his uncle and Aunt Amelia?'

'He is not his uncle. Besides, I am not completely heartless, Delphine. I understand why Amelia fell for Richard Plomley. Not only was he handsome, but also his wife was a shrew—no one could understand why he married her at the time. It can't have been easy being married to a complaining woman who spent most of her time in bed nursing one sickness after another.'

'Does that mean you forgive Aunt Amelia?'

'Things change with time,' he muttered grudgingly. 'But what happened then holds no significance to what is happening now. It is my wish that you marry Lord Beaumont.'

Her heart lurching sickeningly, Delphine left him then, feeling a decade older and a decade sadder than before. She paused at the door and looked back at him, seeing him as she had not seen him in a long time because she had never really looked—a beaten, ailing old man worried for her. Now something in his face caught her. A moment later she knew what it was. Death. This man, her beloved grandfather, who loved her dearly, was dying. Grief rose in her.

'Your mind is made up?' she asked on a gentler note while the thought of her future as the wife of the Master of Pendene was creeping through her veins like spreading ice.

He looked at her long and hard, then he nodded. He was not about to give up, she could see that. He mustered his forces to bring himself under control and brought as much grandparental inflection to his words as he could bring to bear, which told Delphine that her situation was hopeless. 'It is for the best.'

She left him then, catching the lump that had risen in her throat before it could escape.

Her mood angry and tinged with bitterness and disenchantment, Delphine left the house, uncaring in which direction she went, unconsciously heading for the cliff above the cove. There seemed to be nothing she could do to alleviate the troubles that beset her. Her grandfather was determined to sell the land— why had she not thought to ask the value of that land and what he could hope to make from it? Forcing herself to think with cold logic, she knew that whatever he left would be hers since there was no one else. Perhaps it would be enough for her to live on for a while. Then there was Aunt Amelia. Unfortunately she was as poor as a church mouse.

That was the moment when her thoughts turned to Lord Beaumont and she began to question his reason for arriving at Pendene after years without habitation. She had ridden past the house on occasion. It was in a beautiful situation and had been a fine house in its day, but after years of neglect it was in a sorry state.

Having reached the top of the cliff, she saw a man standing looking out to sea, a sombre and magnificent figure in a plain but perfectly tailored midnight-blue frock coat, black breeches above gleaming black riding boots. Delphine felt an iron band tighten suddenly around her heart and there was a taste of ashes in her mouth. For a moment the world seemed to turn upside down. She recognised at once that proud and arrogant form. There could be no mistake. It was indeed the Englishman she had rescued from the Conciergerie.

The shock she received on seeing him again, a man who had made such a tremendous impression on her, a man who had stirred all the feminine desires she thought she would never feel, a man she had never thought to set eyes on again, rendered her speechless and incapable of any coherent thought. Her first instinct was to turn about and run. But in a moment common sense prevailed over the sudden alarm which had taken hold of her. Suddenly, the deep blue sea and the trees and the profusion of gorse bushes seemed to melt away and Delphine was as cold as if she had been miraculously transported into an icy glacier.

As if sensing her presence, he turned and looked at her. Shock and surprise registered on his face and they stood quite still in those first few moments, savouring each other with their eyes. Recognition flowed across his face and surprise and pleasure lit his eyes. There was health and vitality about him that was almost mesmerising. In all, he was even more handsome than she remembered. Happiness soared through her and her heart gave a joyous leap. But too much had been said, too many insults that were still deeply painful for Delphine, too much humiliation remembered for her to succumb once more to this man.

And then she knew. This was the man her grandfather had made his offer to, that he take her along with the parcel of land he coveted. She was shocked to the core. That was the moment her world began to fall apart.

She began to walk towards him, the hem of her daffodil-yellow dress swishing against the grass at her feet. Her body was rigid as she faced him, as if her anger was barely confined. The sun had turned her unbound mane of hair to molten gold and her wonderful amber eyes were liquid bright as they met and clashed with a pair of steely green orbs. Feeling his scorching eyes on her, she found it impossible to greet him with any degree of casualness after the harsh words they had exchanged before they had parted on Guernsey.

'So you are Laurence Beaumont. I am surprised to see you here in Cornwall. Had we parted on better terms I would, in my foolishness, think you had sought me out. However, we would both know that is not the case and that meeting again like this is merely coincidence.'

'Good Lord! I would not have believed... Sophie—'

'Not Sophie—although it is my middle name. I am Delphine and you have just paid a visit to my grandfather, I believe.'

He stiffened, his handsome face seemed to harden and then dissolve into indecision as he, too, realised what was happening. 'You are Jacob Arlington's granddaughter?'

'Yes. You are surprised.'

'I admit it, I am. I had no idea.'

'How could you? Neither of us knew the identity of the other—which was how it had to be.'

His eyes registered pure masculine admiration as his gaze drifted over her. Clearly the effect of seeing her pleased him. 'You look well, Delphine—and as lovely as I remember.' A crooked smile accompanied his compliment.

Resentment coursed through Delphine's veins. He raised his eyes to her face where they captured hers and held them prisoner until she felt a warmth suffuse her cheeks. As handsome as he was, since his return to London and resuming his old life, she could imagine that he had grown quite adept at persuading besotted women to do his bidding.

He did seem to have a way about him and she could not fault any woman for falling under his spell, for she found to her amazement that her heart was not as distantly detached as she might have imagined it to be. Shaking off the effects of what his presence was doing to her, she took herself mentally in hand and reminded herself of their bitter final encounter. Better to remain aloof and save her pride.

'You look well also, Lord Beaumont—your return to London society clearly suits you—and yet here you are in Cornwall. My grandfather tells me you have called on him, that you would like to purchase this land upon which we stand.' He nodded. 'It must disappoint you to know you cannot have the land without taking me with it. What do you think of that?'

'I'm still thinking about it. Would you not prefer to return to the house where we can discuss the matter?'

'No. I prefer to speak of what transpired between the two of you in private, rather than in the house with Grandfather's flapping ears.'

'I see. It sounds ominous.' Completely relaxed, he turned his head and let his gaze sweep over the great expanse of the English Channel and the scenic coastline. 'What a wonderful situation this is,' he said. 'The view from up here is quite spectacular. I had no idea Cornwall was so beautiful.'

Delphine studied his stiff back for a moment longer before she spoke. 'I didn't come here to admire the scenery.'

He turned his head back to her, a slight smile playing on his lips. 'No. I don't expect you did.'

'My grandfather's suggestion that we marry is quite ridiculous. I know you will agree with me absolutely and not even countenance an alliance between us—and I have no wish to marry you—not for land, financial reasons or anything else. How he could have suggested such a thing is quite beyond me. Although since he has no idea what has transpired between us, then he can be forgiven, although I'm afraid he's going to be terribly disappointed.'

Laurence looked her in the eye and smiled, then his face turned sombre again. 'I am sure your grandfather will only do what he considers is best for you.'

'I recall you telling me that most marriages in the world you inhabit are business arrangements. That kind of marriage does not find favour with me—any more than your suggestion that I become your mistress,' she reminded him coldly. She looked at him frankly, with a chilling dispassion.

'Ah—yes,' he replied, having the grace to look shamefaced. 'I didn't handle things particularly well, did I? I wasn't considering your feelings.'

'How can I be expected to marry a man who insulted me and humiliated me as you have done, by asking me to become his mistress?'

'What I said—I'm sorry. You were angry—and rightly so. It was wrong of me and I have no excuse. I appreciate it was a shock to you. I made you an offer in the heat of the moment, when I knew we were parting and in all probability I would never see you again. It was an offer no lady could accept—I realised that as soon as we parted. After all that you had done for me you did not deserve that. You were quite wonderful—a strong woman who knows her own mind. Do not condemn me on that one mistake.'

'I will try not to, but I will tell you now that I do not approve of the deal my grandfather made with you. I will not enter into a marriage of convenience so that you can acquire a parcel of land.'

'No, I didn't think for one minute that you would. I recall you telling me that love is an all-important factor in marriage. Isn't that what all young ladies aspire to?'

She looked at him calmly. 'A man can get love, as you call it, anywhere. He doesn't have to marry for it.'

From under his strong, straight brows, Laurence gave her a quizzical look. 'The same could be said for a woman—that she can love anywhere. She doesn't have to marry for it.'

'That may be true, but the stigma of an affair clings to a woman—as it did my aunt when...'

'When she entered into an affair with my uncle. Yes,' he said, 'I do know all about that, but it has no bearing on now, Delphine.'

'No, it doesn't. We are different people, although in real life, your sex gives you leave to do as you please.' Unwillingly she met his eyes and, seeing him here, relaxed and at home in his surroundings, he was every inch the aloof, elegant Lord of the Manor, master of all he surveyed, but not the parcel of land on which he was standing. 'I've thought about it.'

'Thought about what?'

'My grandfather's offer to you.' She could sense he was wary, that his guard was up and that there was a distance between them. He was watching her closely. She chose directness, calming herself and saying, 'I feel I must tell you that I am not prepared to marry you.'

Not a muscle flickered on Laurence's face. He was silent, looking at her hard, incredulously, as though she had suddenly changed before his eyes. His expression became grim. Folding his arms across his chest, he said, 'Did I ask you?'

Delphine stared at him in sudden confusion, completely thrown by his reply and feeling as if the tables were about to turn on her. His eyes glittered with a fire that turned her raw. The words were uttered without anger, but were none the less cold and final. 'Why—I—no, but I…'

'Then wait until you are asked. Yes, I did approach your grandfather with a request to buy the land and when he informed me that you would have to come with it, I did agree to give the matter my consideration—and I have decided against it. I am not so desperate for the land—although access to the cove I find appealing. When I decide to marry, I prefer to do the asking myself. I am not in the market for a wife, not until I'm ready.'

Delphine turned her face away. Had he exploded with fury and injured vanity she would have understood it better than this deadly quietness which unnerved her.

'May I ask why you think I have any desire to marry you?'

Delphine was beginning to wish the ground would open up and swallow her. 'I—I thought… Oh, I don't know what I thought. It was presumptuous of me.'

'Yes, it was,' he answered, unfolding his arms and adopting a haughty pose. His eyes remained fixed on her face without the trace of a smile to soften their steely expression. 'Just how much did your grandfather tell you about the settlement, Delphine?'

'All of it, I believe.'

'If I agree to his terms, not only the land but Tregannon itself would come as a portion of your dowry. It is a matter of some irritation to me that his proposition would prevent me from choosing my own wife. Over the years I have learned to be wary of marriageable young ladies who were invariably possessed by matchmaking mothers—or in this case, grandfathers—to whom my wealth, before my father gambled it all away, acted as a magnet and I've become adept at walking away.'

'Then I can understand your dilemma.'

'I'm glad you do and I can also understand your anger. It must be galling to know that your grandfather has discussed this with me without consulting you—without considering what your feelings might be. Now your identity has been revealed to me, knowing how proud and stubborn you can be and your views on marriages that are like business transactions, I cannot imagine that you would accept a prospective suitor to put more importance on a parcel of land than on you. Whatever is decided it will have to be thought out carefully—by both of us.' His anger was beginning to melt, but his voice remained hard. 'When I marry I will do the asking. It will be on my terms and it will not be in return for a parcel of land.'

His tone suggested such finality that Delphine turned away. It shouldn't hurt so much, being attached to a parcel of land—lots of dowries came with similar settlements—but it did. 'Yes, it will have to be considered by both of us. I will leave you now. I imagine Grandfather will be expecting you to call with your answer soon.'

She left him then, without waiting for him to reply.

Chapter Seven

Delphine walked briskly, without looking back. When she had left the house she had been angry that all this had been discussed between the two of them without consideration for her feelings, about what she might want, but now she was so confused she didn't know what to think. She knew Laurence a little better than her grandfather, so he wouldn't have known that no one could push Laurence Beaumont into any decision not of his own making.

She had been adamant when she had told him she would not marry him, so why had she felt offended when he had said he didn't want to marry her either? And why, after telling him she didn't want to marry him, did she feel so wretched? Would it be so terrible being his wife? she asked herself. The attraction they felt for each other had been bubbling away below the surface ever since they had met in Paris.

All these thoughts tumbled over and over themselves in her mind until she didn't know what to think

any more or what she should do. From the moment
she had taken it into her head not to even consider
marrying Laurence and then doubting her decision
just now, without warning, she felt as if she was being
swept off her feet by a strong current borne along by
a great, silent force over which she had no control—
only to come back down to earth with a thud.

Laurence watched her walk away, thinking it a
strange twist of fate that had brought him to Cornwall
and Delphine. Of course she would be feeling upset
and his conscience tore at him. Better to let things
settle down, but he was beginning to regret ever approaching Jacob Arlington as much as he regretted
suggesting that she become his mistress.

He continued to watch her, observing the swish of
her skirts as she walked along. She looked as healthy
and thoughtless as a young animal, sleek, graceful
and as high-spirited as a thoroughbred, and dangerous when crossed. There was also a subdued strength
and subtleness that gave her an easy, almost naive elegance she was totally unaware of.

Though he had once thought himself immune to
the subtle ploys of women, even though he had known
Delphine for such a short time, he had begun to think
he would never be free of her. From the beginning
she had stirred his baser instincts. Yet much as she
ensnared his thoughts, he found his dreams daunting
to his manly pride, for she flitted through them like
some puckish sprite. Although he'd have preferred
to limit her constant assault on his thoughts and his

poorly depleted restraint, he was beginning to suspect that, in comparison, standing firm against the Parisian mob had been child's play.

The sun shone directly on the glossy cape of her golden hair which had escaped the restriction of the ribbon as she walked. Few women were fortunate enough to have been blessed with such captivating looks. In fact, Delphine was blessed with everything she would need to guarantee her future happiness. The sheer beauty of her caught his breath, then irritation bloomed at her recklessness in roaming through the countryside alone like some wandering, beautiful gypsy.

Turning to his horse and grasping the reins, he swung himself up into the saddle. He had much to think about before he went to visit Jacob Arlington. One thing he was sure of: he wanted Delphine more than he had wanted anything in his life before and, despite their harsh words, he was determined to find a way to resolve the situation before too long.

It was to be two days before the two of them saw each other again. Delphine had ridden into Fowey to see Aunt Amelia. The wind ruffled her hair, tugging it loose from the blue ribbon. Her dog, a faithful companion when on her rides, raced ahead. He was a large dog called Finn, young and fresh and relieved to be out of the stables, his sleek black shape pouring over the ground and slipping in and out of the rocks. Above the town, she paused, looking down into the bustling harbour. She dismounted and left her horse to nibble the short grass.

Sitting on the grey-veined rocks, she clasped her arms around her drawn-up knees, the dog settling beside her. The air was sweet, smelling of the spiky bushes of gorse and tasting of the sea. Her gaze travelled over the vessels at anchor on the bay, some sleek and fast with tall masts pointing to the sky and sails neatly furled.

She saw a young girl in a blue dress, with the brim of a sun bonnet shading her face, walking up from the town and pausing some way away from her, as if waiting for someone. The girl suddenly came to life when a young man seemed to appear from nowhere and take hold of her, spinning her round. The girl squealed with delight and when he placed her back on the ground, her cheeks flushed a charming pink as she accepted his proffered arm. Delphine stared in fascination as the sweethearts walked off, heading away from the town towards the woods.

Delphine tried to imagine how it would be to have someone like that young man, someone to welcome her with such doting affection and tender love. She'd had little time to envision herself as a wife and having a family of her own, but at that moment she envied that young woman her doting young man.

Her thoughts far away, she did not hear the approach of another rider. Looking up and shielding her eyes against the sun's brightness, she saw a man astride a horse looking down at her. Her eyes and brain recognised his presence, but her emotions were slow to follow.

'Laurence!' she said, surprised to see him.

Mocking green eyes gazed back at her. 'Aye, Delphine,' he said, swinging his powerful frame out of the saddle, his boots sounding sharp against the stones on the path. 'My apologies. I didn't mean to startle you.'

Removing his hat, he looked down at her, his face grave, though Delphine noticed one eyebrow was raised in that whimsical way he had and his lips were inclined to curl in a smile. What was he doing here? She had time to wonder, since he was a long way from Pendene.

His gaze swept the landscape, settling for just a moment on the skeletal masts in the bay, before coming to rest on Delphine, who made no attempt to get up. If he was surprised to see that she wore a jacket and breeches and black riding boots more suitable to a male than a female, he didn't show it. With her arm resting on her drawn-up knee, she lounged indolently against the rock at her back.

'Does your grandfather not worry that you ride about the countryside unattended?'

Raising her eyebrow as if surprised by his question, she looked up at him. 'Not in the least. If I can travel the roads of France while it is at war without a companion, then Cornwall is nothing to complain about.'

'My dear Delphine! If your grandfather knew of your clandestine activities, I imagine he would have much to say about it. Besides, you had Jacques to take care of you in France.'

'We worked together. Here I have my faithful companion,' she said, fondling the dog's silken ears. 'His name is Finn. He is gentle and affectionate, but let anyone make a move against me he doesn't like and he can become as fierce as a tiger.' She scowled at him. 'And I am not your dear.'

A soft chuckle and a warm, appreciative light in his eyes conveyed his pleasure. 'You are by far the loveliest and dearest thing I have seen for many a year, Delphine.'

A lazy smile dawned across his face and Delphine's heart skipped a beat. Laurence Beaumont had a smile that could melt an iceberg. She immediately wished she'd worn her riding habit, which was less revealing than her breeches, for his careful scrutiny left no curve untouched. His unswerving gaze became fixed on her lithesome figure. At the sight of her hips and long, slim legs, outlined with anatomical precision by the close-fitting breeches, a crooked smile crossed his face and a low whistle passed between his lips.

'Good Lord!' He chuckled. 'What a strange turnout!'

When his eyes returned to hers, her cheeks were aflame with embarrassment. He smiled into her eyes. 'I often ride in breeches,' she told him. 'They're far more comfortable than a skirt.' He gave her such a long, deliciously wicked perusal that it took her breath away and increased the colour in her cheeks.

'I won't argue with that. You really are quite lovely, you know.'

'And you are the most insufferable man I have ever met.' The words were uttered without rancour.

She fell silent, looking at him openly. His face was virile with a compelling strength, which said that no matter what words were flung at him, he would never yield to them. His dark curling hair was tied back, glossy and thick, dipping across his wide forehead. His eyes, a deep brilliant green, were steady and narrowed when he smiled and his mobile mouth curved across strong white teeth.

'What are you doing in Fowey?' she asked.

'I've been to see someone concerning the mine I've inherited and I'm on my way back to Pendene. And you, Delphine? What are you doing here?' he asked, perching on a rock beside her.

'I'm going to see my aunt.'

'I'm glad I've run into you.'

'Are you? Why?'

'Because we need to reach an understanding before too long. Don't you agree? Your grandfather's proposition cannot be ignored. Harsh words were spoken when we last met. Now we've had time to consider everything, perhaps we could make a decision without his influence—to decide what would suit us.'

Tilting her head to one side, Delphine considered him with a thoughtful look. 'What are you saying, Laurence? That you have changed your mind about not wanting to marry me?'

'I don't recall saying I didn't want to marry you.

Initially I would not entertain the idea, since I found it distasteful that your grandfather made sure to impress on me that you and the land came together. I refused to be browbeaten by a wily old man eager to foist his granddaughter on me for a patch of land. But now I know the identity of the lady in question—and after much quiet contemplation—I think it's an interesting idea and one you and I might examine at more leisure.'

'So, in order to get your hands on that parcel of land, you might be prepared to take me along with it after all.' She sighed. 'It does nothing for my ego. I'm sorry. He is trying to do his best for me.'

'You must realise that you will have to marry eventually.'

'Must? No, I do not. I never considered myself wifely material, and quite unfit for the role to be any man's wife—although that doesn't mean I'm against marriage—quite the opposite, in fact. Settling down in a loving marriage with a husband and children appeals to me. Taking into account my grandfather's age and his health and the fact that he is quite penniless, there is nowhere else for me to go, so I might as well adhere to his wishes. Should we agree to marry, there is the house, which will come to you as part of my dowry on my grandfather's demise, but it's in need of extensive repairs and I would have no income to maintain it should I not marry you.'

'You have your aunt here in Fowey. You could always move in with her.'

'My *great*-aunt—who happens to be nearly as old as my grandfather and no better off than he is.'

'And you will have to look to the future—to the day when they are both gone and you are alone. I'm beginning to realise that marriage to each other would be advantageous to us both. You cannot blame your grandfather for wanting to make sure you will be settled.'

Delphine thought of the work she had been doing for the past two years and a chill slithered over her. 'I never look or plan beyond the present.'

'I told you. I am prepared to forfeit the land, to remove it from the equation altogether. Although if we were to marry, then it would inevitably come as part of your dowry, so however you look at it, it will still be there.' He glanced at her, his expression serious. 'As my wife you should have no complaints, Delphine.'

'I would hope not—although my survival instincts are well honed. If I were to abide by my grandfather's wishes and become your wife, there will be times when I might have to be absent, which I hope you would not object to.'

He glanced at her sharply. 'You would not give up your trips to France?'

'It is important to me that I carry on. There will be those wanting to escape the terror for a long time yet—and I have yet to find my father.'

His eyes narrowed and his mouth became a grim line of perilous determination. 'There is no one more aware of the dangers of your work than I. I would not be in favour of you doing that. As my wife I would have to insist that you abandon that idea.' He said it reasonably enough, quietly enough, but the meaning behind his words was plain.

'No, I don't imagine you would be,' she said, her expression telling him that she could be determined, too, and her own face was rigid in its stubbornness. Her eyes had changed from their usual soft amber to the spark and fire of a different hue. There was a spot of colour at each cheekbone and her mouth was as thinly drawn with determination as her future husband's.

'I intend to curtail my work for the present— because of Grandfather's failing health, you understand, but eventually I must continue my search for my father. You must also understand that I will continue to spend time with my aunt, so you must not feel you have to entertain me. I am capable of occupying my own time.'

'I have no objection to that. But going back to France is another matter entirely, one I cannot support.'

She looked away. The air between them had become charged with something she did not like. 'I am sorry to hear that,' she said, her expression ready to tell him she would not be ordered about. 'Nothing has been decided between us yet, Laurence. It is something that can be considered later—should we wed, that is.'

She held her head up in defiance and for a moment she saw a glimmer of something in Laurence's eyes which, had she not known better, she might have called admiration. He stood up and stepped away from her, his attention on the sea spread out before him, and something about the maddening swagger of his confident gait raised her ire. What had started out as a mission to rescue him from the Conciergerie had turned into something else entirely, something quite different from anything she could have imagined.

'What has made you come to Cornwall?' she asked, considering it prudent to change the subject and her curiosity to know more about him coming to the fore. 'It's a long way from London and so very different.'

'I am to sell my London house and decided to live at Pendene.'

'But—will you not miss London?'

'No. There is nothing for me there. I will not dwell on the past and concentrate instead on the Pendene estate.' He turned and looked at her. 'Don't think too badly of your grandfather. People do desperate things when times are bad. He loves you. It is important for him to know you will be safe and taken care of.'

'But I shouldn't be thinking of marrying you or anyone else—until…'

'Until your father comes back,' he said quietly.

'Yes. It's weeks since my last mission and already I've fallen into the pattern of living an everyday life, yet I keep thinking, hoping, that maybe, one day soon, he will come back.' She didn't look away as she held his gaze.

'But if he's in some prison in France he's as good as dead—if he's not already.'

'And yet you survived,' she said sharply. 'You came back.'

'Yes, I did. I was an exception—and unlike your father I was not a French aristocrat.'

With the light breeze blowing in from the sea lifting her heavy mane of hair, Delphine got to her feet and stood silently. He was saying things she didn't want to hear. She wanted to hear that with hope and patience her father would come back. She struggled to keep the despair from her face and eyes, and it wasn't possible. This man who was watching her so carefully with those penetrating green eyes that could turn so quickly to the colour of a tropical sea, knew as well as she did what thoughts were hers, how she might never know the fate of her beloved father.

She looked at him. 'He isn't dead. He is still alive. I know it. I feel it in my heart. While ever I am here he will find me.'

'If you become my wife I will not take you away from here. Don't sacrifice your life waiting for something that might never happen. It will take your youth, Delphine—and the beauty of you.'

She didn't rebuke him for his negativity, nor did she attempt a denial of his words. 'Which means nothing to me until I know. You really have made up your mind to remain in Cornwall?'

He nodded. 'I no longer have any desire to live in London. I want to be where there's air to breathe and in summer to feel the sun on my bones.'

'Why do you want to buy the land from my grandfather? Could it possibly be that the cove is the attraction?' she asked with a note of amusement.

He grinned. 'You read me too well. The cove is important since I want access to the sea.'

'The land would be a valuable asset to anyone with smuggling in mind. It does have access to a series of coves, one of them large enough to conceal a boat and contraband that would be difficult to find. The surrounding cliffs hide the existence of the small natural harbour just round the corner from a promontory. Following a shipwreck years ago when a whole crew and passengers went down with the ship, people avoided the cove, believing it to be cursed. That is an advantage to smugglers. It has a sandy beach and a foreshore that gives easy access to the land.'

'I like the story about it being cursed. All the better. I would have it all to myself.'

'So—you would become a smuggler—a dishonest occupation—although Cornish people consider cheating the King's Revenue a way of life, not a crime.'

He laughed. 'Then I will become a Cornishman and adopt the attitude and views of my neighbours. But if I were to turn my hand to such a nefarious occupation, then I shall also keep the Revenue Men happy by paying my dues now and then. I also appear to have inherited a defunct mine. I need money to put my plans I'm working on into action—hence the sale of the London house. There will be changes here. For years the estate has been just ticking over. I intend to put the land to the best use. I want to make Pendene an example of excellence of how an estate should be in Cornwall. I'm also considering reopening the mine which my uncle closed twenty years ago.'

Delphine was deeply moved by his obvious enthusiasm for his plans and all he wanted to achieve. 'Is there still copper there?'

'I have been told by reliable sources that there are substantial deposits of copper down there, seams that have never been mined. I am aware of the process involved to get the mine working again and becoming financially successful. If I am to reopen it, I am going to need money to do that, so being an adventurer and a man used to taking risks, the money I am tempted to make from smuggling will be put to good use—to getting the mine working again. When I eventually reopen it, it will provide work for families hereabouts.'

'I thought—I had the impression that you were rich.'

'Unfortunately I am not. My father was a gambler, Delphine. He would lay bets on anything that moved—be it the back of a horse or a fly climbing up a wall. There was no stopping him. And then when there was nothing left, he died. So,' he said, turning away from her and looking out to sea, 'I have decided to sell the house in London and move to Cornwall for good. I will inject some of the money I make from the sale into the mine and hopefully it will become profitable once more.'

'Do you have knowledge of how a mine works?'

'Not much, but I have been educated enough to leave me with a mind that is ready to absorb new things and new ideas. All I have to do is get the money to make it work.'

Delphine could not see his face, but she saw the hands clasped behind his back tighten. 'What a couple of paupers we are. And money is important to you?'

Suddenly he spoke fiercely, still with his back to her. 'Isn't it to everyone? I'm not ashamed to like money. It's what makes the world tick. I like it and for a man who has stared death in the face every day for a whole year in the Conciergerie—until a delightful young lady came to get me out, I might add—then I want to live, Delphine. I want all this,' he said with a deep and abiding passion Delphine had never heard before.

He spread his arms wide to encompass the sea and the land around him. 'Fortunes do change. I want enjoyment in my life—not misery or the falsities of life in London. Here I will be free—and ten years from now the Conciergerie will be just a distant memory.'

In the moment of silence which fell between them, Delphine was able to take stock of what he had just told her. 'And your work with the Intelligence Service?'

Laurence turned and looked at her. His eyes were as calm as the sea on a fair day. 'I'm done with all that. I have served in the service for too many years. I was well trained in the physical art of weaponry, but I was also trained in manipulation and deception and seeking out information valuable to the government in the war not only with France, but with America, too.

'Keeping people at arm's length became second nature—as was the secrecy, the isolation. The punishing regimes in discipline of body and mind toughened one up for whatever lay ahead—diverse lessons turning agents into good spies as well as killers. I will not be caught up in it again. I want to be free of it.' He looked at her. 'Do you understand what I am saying?'

Delphine was stirred by the depth of passion in his voice. He stood very still, but it seemed to her that his broad shoulders drooped and bowed, as though under the force of some strong feeling. Had she been wrong about him all along? Was Laurence Beaumont more of a gentleman than she had first given him credit for?

'Yes—yes, I do. You cannot go on playing the gentleman without a penny in your pocket.'

'Which is why I'm doing this. Now, I realise there will be difficulties—and even in the short time I have been here, I have had doubts about what I'm doing. But it's a challenge, Delphine. It's what I need right now.'

'When you put it like that I cannot fault you.'

'So,' he said, moving closer to her and looking down at her upturned face, 'what shall we tell your grandfather? I told him I would consider his offer and call back.'

'Let him wait. It's not something that can be decided in a hurry. And…' she said, lowering her eyes, 'I would appreciate it if you don't let him know we have met before today. It would take some explaining and he wouldn't understand.'

He nodded. 'You have my word.'

'Thank you.'

'I'm riding out to take a look at the mine tomorrow. Would you care to accompany me?'

'Yes, I would like that.'

'Good. That's settled then. We'll meet at the top of the cove at ten o'clock if that suits you.'

'Yes. I'll look forward to it. But—what are you doing now? Are you returning to Pendene?'

'Yes. We could ride back together.'

'Would you like to meet my aunt?'

He looked surprised. 'I hadn't thought about it. Would she like to see me?'

'I don't see why not.'

'What is she like? Need I be worried?'

Delphine laughed. 'She can be a bit of a dragon, but I'm sure you'll be safe enough—especially being the nephew of her adored Richard Plomley.'

They arrived at a street which rose up inland. Laurence tied up his horse and Delphine told the dog to stay. He whined at the thought of being left and to soothe him she stroked his shining head and caressed his ears, to the dog's evident delight, and she was rewarded by the thump of a black tail. Watching her with considerable amusement, Laurence could see the animal meant a great deal to her the way she was fussing over it. He felt a strange sensation come over him and he could hardly believe it when he realised it was resentment—that he, Laurence Beaumont, who knew himself to be attractive to women, could be jeal-

ous of a dog. It flopped down beside the horse and
Laurence was certain it would be in the same place
when their visit was over.

Delphine knocked on one of the doors. It was
opened by a fresh-faced young woman. Her face lit
up when she saw Delphine.

'Why, Miss Delphine, your aunt will be right
pleased to see you.'

'How is she, Ruth?'

'She's not been too good this week. Keeps having
dizzy spells. I tell her she's overdoing it—what with
ladies calling all day and she going visiting, but will
she listen? You know what she's like. She has diffi-
culty getting about, but that's her arthritis.'

Delphine laughed. 'I certainly do, Ruth. And you
know she will not be told.'

They followed Ruth into the parlour which overlooked the street. There was a fire burning in the
hearth even though it was a summer's day. Delphine
went and kissed her aunt, who was sitting by the window in a comfortable chair watching the world go by.
Introductions were made and Aunt Amelia couldn't
hide her surprise that Laurence was the nephew of
Richard Plomley and that he had inherited Pendene.

'You are a handsome young man,' she said with
a smile, 'and you do bear a resemblance to Richard. Being handsome is always an asset in life—for
prince or pauper.'

Laurence sat and listened to the exchange of conversation between Delphine and her aunt. As he listened, after a while he was aware that the elderly

lady's thoughts were elsewhere and he maintained a discreet silence, sipping at his tea to pass the time while Delphine chatted on in the way families do. But then Amelia's eyes settled on him.

'I'm sorry, Lord Beaumont. I allowed my thoughts to wander. It was very rude of me. It's just that you being here takes me back. Having you here in this house reminds me of when Richard used to visit.'

Laurence looked at the face of Delphine's aunt, at the bright eyes, the fine bone formation of her face and slender form, and he realised that she had once been a great beauty. Little wonder his uncle had fallen for her.

As if reading his thoughts she looked at him directly and he saw a certain sadness behind the smile which quickly changed to mischievousness. 'That was a long time ago,' she said, leaving Laurence to wonder how she could have known what he was thinking.

'Now, tell me what you are doing here, visiting an old lady together? I was young once, and I can see when two people are—well—you know what I'm saying. Is there something going on between the two of you that I should know about?'

Delphine laughed and told her about what had transpired between Laurence and her grandfather.

'Still, he must have his reasons—and—he must like you, Lord Beaumont.'

'As to that I cannot say,' Laurence answered. 'We've only met the once.'

'First impressions are important and he clearly

found you favourable. If you are anything like Richard, then the two of you will do well together.'

'And you know that, do you, Aunt Amelia?' Delphine said, a smile on her lips as she looked at her aunt.

'One gets wiser as one gets older and therefore that is what I am, my dear. I know what I see. Delphine is like me, Lord Beaumont, and her mother before her when she took it into her head to marry her French count. She will not be idle, you can count on that.' She looked at Delphine. 'Have you heard anything about your father, Delphine? Has there been word of what might have happened to him?'

'No, Aunt Amelia. But I continue to make enquiries. If he is still alive, then I will find him.'

Under the mischievousness, Laurence detected a will of iron in Delphine's aunt and he suspected that past events had served to forge this strength. He knew he would have to be careful how he dealt with Delphine in the future. Her remark that she would continue looking for her father should serve as a warning to him. If Delphine set her mind to something, Laurence felt she would be difficult to stop.

They talked some more and when Ruth came to inform her that two of her lady friends had arrived to take tea with her, Delphine stood up and embraced her.

'We'll go now, Aunt Amelia. We've taken up too much of your time already. Thank you for the tea.'

'I'm glad you came. It was so nice to meet you, Lord Beaumont. You must get Delphine to bring you again soon.'

* * *

When he had left Delphine close to Tregannon, Laurence rode back to Pendene, having been given much to think about. The fate of Pendene, with its surrounding land and two farms, lay in his hands. In all the estate extended to six hundred acres. The Pendene and Tregannon land neighboured each other, some of the Tregannon land on the north side having been sold to Pendene over the years and the rest to neighbouring landowners on the west. The only land Jacob Arlington had held on to was the ten acres with access to the cove.

After much soul searching as to the wisdom of what he was doing, offering marriage to Delphine, he decided it was the right thing to do. Since his arrest in France and facing imminent death on a daily basis, he'd had time to consider his past life. On returning to London he was plagued by a deep awareness of his situation. There was a hole in his life, an emptiness. He had sensed it before he had embarked on the dangerous occupation as a government agent, but since arriving back in England it had sharpened into a nameless hunger to put things right.

As yet his sisters had produced only daughters. He needed heirs, which meant finding a wife, a prospect he little relished until he had something to offer other than a title, be it the minor one of baron. Now the old man, Jacob Arlington, had offered him his granddaughter, a young woman, he had said, who could take care of herself. The old man had made a favourable impression on him and yet anger welled up inside him against the man, and also against himself for being unable to turn his back on what he had offered, possibly at the price of his granddaughter's happiness.

Delphine's impact on him was powerful. She was young and vulnerable and, despite her quality of mind to show self-possession, how ripe she was for being initiated into the secret, mysterious paths of womanhood. And yet, this aside, the absolute courage of what she had done in France proved she had a strong will and determination to achieve what she set out to do, and she did that in silence, with no praise, no accolade for a job well done. Her missions were of extreme danger in defence of national security in these troubled times, although he was aware that her contribution to the war effort was to find her father.

In practical terms she would make an ideal wife. She was caring and capable and her capacity for loyalty was unquestioned, having doted on her father and her grandfather all her life. She was also extremely beautiful and his admiration for her was beyond doubt. She deserved privilege and a life of ease more than any woman he knew. At this time he could not offer her that, but as his wife she would be able to continue to live in Cornwall.

It was over dinner with her grandfather that Delphine casually dropped her meeting with Laurence in Fowey into the conversation. His eyes snapped open with sudden interest.

'And? What did you think of him? Did you like him?'

'Yes,' she admitted. 'I like him as well as it is possible on a first meeting.'

Her admission seemed to gratify him. 'Well, that's
a start. He made a favourable impression on me and
I sincerely hoped you would like him.'

'Aunt Amelia liked him. She told me he reminded
her of his uncle.'

Her grandfather stopped eating and stared at her
incredulously. 'You—you took him to see Amelia?'

She nodded. 'Why not? I was going to see her anyway and I didn't think it would do any harm.'

'And?'

'She was impressed.'

'Well—that's something I suppose. I think we
should invite him to Tregannon so you can get to
know him better.'

'Later. He's invited me to ride out with him tomorrow—he wants to show me Pendene.'

'Did you accept?'

'Yes,' she said nonchalantly shrugging her shoulders. 'Why not? I've nothing else to do. Besides, I've
always wanted to see inside Pendene.'

Chapter Eight

Wearing a blue riding habit and a broad-brimmed hat to shield her face from the sun, Delphine went to the stable to saddle her dappled grey mare straight after breakfast. Finn met her, wagging his tail excitedly, ready to accompany her on her ride. She was nervous—this surprised her, for she was always in control of her emotions. She didn't want to be early for her meeting with Laurence, yet she didn't want to be late, not wanting to waste a moment that was hers to spend with him.

But what if he didn't come?

She needn't have worried. He was there waiting, when the sun had not had time to burn the dew off the grass. Riding astride, she gave the impression that she was a woman of tireless energy and spent the best part of her time in the saddle.

Laurence turned when she appeared, giving her a smile that was light-hearted and welcoming. 'Good morning, Delphine, and what a lovely sight you are.

It's refreshing to see a young lady who defies convention and casts decorum to the four winds by riding alone and astride.'

She laughed, feeling all the joys of an early ride with a handsome man by her side. 'I cast decorum and convention aside long ago.'

'You ride well—although I would expect nothing less of you. Nice horse, by the way.'

'The pride of my grandfather's stable,' she replied, leaning forward and caressing her horse's neck. 'In fact, she's the only horse in my grandfather's stable. The others have been long gone.'

'Speaking of your grandfather—have you told him that we arranged to meet?'

'Yes—although I must tell you that he's wondering why you haven't been to call on him with your decision regarding the land—and myself, of course.'

For an instant some of his good humour seemed to have deserted him. He took the reins and mounted his horse with an easy swing, his frock coat swirling about his legs. 'He'll have to wait until I'm ready—and you, of course. There is much to consider—for both of us. I will do nothing you do not approve of. Now,' he said, looking ahead, 'let's blow some cobwebs away.'

In moments they had left the cove behind. With Finn scampering on ahead of them, they let their horses stretch out, sweeping along the open land at a gallop. Delphine gloried in the taste of freedom she always experienced on her rides. The sun shone brightly and she laughed aloud at the thrill of it all, the hoofbeats pounding the turf like a drum.

They rode past meadows where sheep cropped the grass, disturbing a flock of birds up from some scrub and sending a clutch of rabbits darting for cover. When the going became more difficult they rode further inland, taking their time and following paths Delphine had ridden many times. It was pleasant riding through woods in deep shade, where a stream meandered slowly along before its final gallop to the sea.

When they reached the mine, a sad, melancholy air hung over the granite engine house and empty mine buildings. Ladders, still in their places in the open shaft, led down to complete and utter darkness, to the secret heart of the mine. Mother Nature had long since claimed the ground and burrows of waste, which had once blighted the landscape and offended the eye. All were reminders of what had once been.

Dismounting they walked towards the engine house. Butterflies and bumblebees drifted about above the tall meadow grass and wild flowers. It was hot in the sun. Delphine followed in Laurence's wake as he walked about, taking it all in.

'It's in quite a state,' he murmured after a while, looking around and shoving a discarded bucket out of his path with his boot. On a sigh he looked at the dilapidation around him. 'As you see, Delphine, there is much to be done if I'm going to get it up and working. But I do believe, I feel it in my bones, that this could be a highly profitable mine. I have discussed it at length with my estate manager, John McGuire, who tells me that to mine in the direction the copper deposits lie, I may have to sink another shaft—which adds to the cost. I will also bring in the experts to make an inspection.'

'How soon can you sell your London house?'

'Soon, I hope. I don't think that will be a problem. I will have to return to London to set the wheels in motion.'

'You really are serious about doing this, aren't you, Laurence?'

'Absolutely. I really do believe I would be doing the right thing coming to live down here. But what of us, Delphine? If we decide to accept your grandfather's offer, how would you feel?'

'Do you mean about becoming your wife?' she asked faintly, staring at him, an uneasy note in her soft tone.

'Exactly.'

'I can't say that I am flattered by the manner of it—in fact, it—it's humiliating to even think I come as part and parcel with ten acres of land. I love my grandfather dearly, but it seems to me I am as much his property as the land.'

'You are no man's property.' Laurence smiled, his expression softening.

'I'm glad you think so, but that does not alter the fact that you cannot have one without the other—or, at least, you cannot have the land without me.'

'You do me an injustice, Delphine. I am not nearly as mercenary as you make me out to be.'

'No,' she conceded. 'Perhaps not. But I cannot help

remembering the conversation we had when you referred to society weddings as being a business transaction between the two families involved, where the couple come together like polite strangers. Marriage between us would feel like that, which is something that does not sit comfortably with me.'

'I should have explained that not all marriages are like that. Some couples do marry for love, and when marriages are arranged for the benefit of the families involved, then the couple often do come to love one another. I do believe your grandfather has only your happiness and welfare at heart, as I do. On the other hand, you are of age to do as you please, marry anyone you please.'

'I know. But I have to admit that there are advantages for me if I were to marry you. I couldn't remain at Tregannon since I could not afford the upkeep—unless,' she said, a smile playing on her lips, a mischievous, almost wicked smile, 'I were to throw in my hand with the smugglers and allow them use of the cove. I might even consider becoming a smuggler myself—imagine the shock and the scandal that would cause.'

He laughed. 'There is that. Why don't you?'

'It doesn't appeal to me. It's a male-dominated occupation and they wouldn't accept me.'

'Wouldn't you like to be involved in the trade?'

'I would have to give it some thought before I did.' Tilting her head sideways, she gave him a hard look. 'I hope you do not share the common failing of most men, Laurence, and suffer from the masculine illusion that women do not have heads for business, that they should be guided by the superior knowledge of men and have no opinions of their own, and—in particular—have no place in the trade.'

'Heaven forbid I should think that,' he answered, his teeth gleaming as his bold eyes laughed down into hers, 'and if I did, I would not dare say so. I like a woman who speaks her mind and I know through personal knowledge of you that you are not only beautiful, but courageous, too.'

Delphine flushed, so surprised by the compliment that she was thrown off balance, but then she checked herself. 'Careful, Laurence. Flattery will not get you what you want—be it the land or myself without I give it some consideration. However, marriage to you would mean that I wouldn't have to leave here—I consider this my home, you see, since I have no connection to France any more. And should my father come back, then this is where he will come to find me.'

'So you would consider becoming my wife? I am serious about this, Delphine. It matters a great deal to me what you want,' he told her softly. 'I do want you. I would always keep you safe, I promise you.'

'You can't promise that.'

'I can. I'm very determined.'

His face was calm and he sounded so sure of himself. He spoke the words quietly. His eyes weren't easy to read. He said he wanted her and he was a man who never spoke anything but the truth.

'Do you mean,' she said carefully, 'that you would marry me without the land?'

'Yes, I do. I cannot say it any other way. If there was some other way, I would say it.'

Delphine wanted him to say it in every way it was possible to say. She wanted it said over and over again. She wanted it with all the intimacies of two people in love. But it was not that time for them—not yet.

She looked at him and saw all the things that attracted her to him. She saw the darkly handsome face of the man whose life she had saved. She saw his body, his height and his strength. She knew his honesty and felt his need to succeed in all he set out to do. But she did not know the inner core of him, to touch the passion in him. This was what she wanted and in time, if she were to become his wife, she would see it.

Seeing her indecision, he shook his head. 'I know it's not much I'm offering you. All I can see is hard work ahead. I'm not saying it will be easy because I know it will be anything but. It's the kind of journey I never imagined I would make. I am asking you to come with me on that journey. It needs a special kind of woman to do that.'

'I'm not special, Laurence, and after seeing the worst that can happen to people, I know I could do this. But I do not want to be reminded of what I did in France—and that you are trying to pay it back. I couldn't bear that. I don't want you to ask me to be your wife because you think you owe it to me—out of some kind of obligation.'

'If you think that, then you really do not know me.'

Leaning negligently against a tree, he folded his arms across his chest, watching Delphine in speculative silence through narrowed eyes. He had removed his coat and loosened his neckcloth, and beneath the soft linen shirt his muscles flexed with any slight movement he made. He exuded hard strength and posed with leashed sensuality, a hard set to his jaw and a cynicism in his bright green eyes. But then he smiled, lazily and devastatingly, his teeth as white as his neckcloth.

Delphine removed her hat and the breeze blew her hair across her face. She reached up and absently drew it back, combing her fingers through it and sweeping it behind her ears, unconscious of how seductive the gesture was to Laurence. He stood absolutely still, watching her with a look that was possessive. Delphine looked at him and something in his expression made her flush and catch her breath, dropping her arm self-consciously. The moment was intimate, warm and vibrantly alive. His vitality at such close quarters alarmed her, but she did not move away.

'No,' she uttered quietly as he held her gaze with her own. 'I don't know you, Laurence—not really.'

'We can soon remedy that.' Taking her hand, he drew her close. Lowering his head, he skimmed his lips over hers. 'Delphine, I would like to kiss you.'

'You would?'

'Yes. Do you mind?'

'I didn't mind when you kissed me on Guernsey and nothing has changed,' she murmured, focusing on his lips as they came closer.

Placing his lips firmly on hers, he kissed her, long and deep. Her lips were soft and pliant and she kissed him back, which deepened the enchantment. She sighed, yielding to the coaxing pressure of his lips parting hers. When she opened her mouth uncertainly, he accepted the invitation with ease. Raising his hands, he stroked the sides of her neck with his thumbs, ruling her senses and knowing she was under the spell of his kiss.

Delphine was too carried away to do anything but let him kiss her. His hand slipped behind her neck and with tantalising slowness he caressed her lips. Naive and inexperienced, she acted purely on instinct, responding naturally to his tender assault on her lips— and it was not just her lips that began to open and respond, but her whole body as they clung to each other, becoming caught up in a wave of pleasure.

Delphine was seduced by his mouth, becoming captive to his touch, his caress and the promise of things to come, secret, mysterious things that set her body trembling. She didn't know what was happening to her. No one had told her what happened when men and women were intimate together. An inexperienced girl could not have imagined such a kiss. She had only ever been kissed by Laurence and to be kissed like this for the second time was devastating. The feelings he aroused in her, with his lips, his touch, his eyes, were irrational, nameless.

Eventually he released her lips, looking down into her upturned face, into her eyes that were large and warm with passion. He smiled. 'There. I think we know each other a little better now. We know each other better than many couples who marry. We became well acquainted on our journey out of France. Please don't ask me to believe that you don't feel the attraction between us,' he said with a faint half-smile. She stood rooted in front of him, as if unable to pull away when he gently traced the curve of her cheek with the backs of his fingers. 'I now know how sensitive you are, how you respond to just a little tender persuasion.'

His words brought a crimson flush to Delphine's cheeks. 'Perhaps you are right. How would I know when I lack your worldly experience? But I have a strong mind, Laurence, and I am not so easily seduced when it comes to making a decision about my future.'

'And the future of those whose lives you save. I would trust you with my life. The risk you take for others, the fear you must live under until your mission is accomplished successfully, I cannot begin to imagine. With everything that has happened since I returned to England—my decision to remove myself from London permanently, the difficulties that face me here at Pendene—I could never have imagined such a time when I was incarcerated in the Conciergerie, expecting to be executed at any time. Where you are concerned I feel—lost. It is not a comfortable feeling for a man who has always known who he is, what he wants in life and where he is going. I am not unaware how difficult the decision as to whether or not to marry me is for you to make.'

'It is—for both of us, not knowing if we are doing the right thing.'

Taking her by the shoulders, he turned her towards

him, his eyes serious and surprisingly understanding.
'Whatever your decision, Delphine,' he said softly,
speaking her name with an intimacy that already had
them attached, his eyes penetrating as they held hers,
'I am on your side. Please believe that.'

'Yes, I believe you are.'

He looked at her for a long moment, reaching up
and brushing her cheek slowly and gently with the
back of his fingers, sending a disconcerting tremor
of warm pleasure coursing through her and causing
her heart to skip a beat, knowing full well that she
was in danger of succumbing to his fatal charm—as
no doubt he was certain she would. She made no effort to move away. As Laurence looked into her eyes
his own were tender and she trembled once more. His
fingers were warm and strong, gently massaging her
cheek, and she felt a sudden urge to turn her head and
kiss the palm of his hand.

'You are under no obligation to marry me, Delphine, but I sincerely hope you will. So, what do you
say? Will you be my wife? Will you marry me and
live at Pendene? It will not be easy, I admit that. But
I do believe that together we can make this work.'

Delphine returned his gaze, her expression as serious as his. His voice was deep and incredibly sin-
cere. She was deeply moved by his words, spoken
seriously and without arrogance. But they did not iron
away all the difficulties facing them. If she married
him it would always be what it was—a marriage of
convenience.

His eyes continued to hold hers and his lips curved

in a quiet smile. She gazed up at him and a long moment passed before she replied. 'Yes, I believe we could,' she said softly. She stepped back from him, afraid of the turmoil inside her, afraid of the weakening effect he was having on her emotions and the enormity of the decision she had made. Laurence took her hand, as if he could sense what she was thinking.

'You are an extremely beautiful and desirable young woman—and please do not accuse me of flattering you in order to seduce you into marriage. The statement is completely true and spoken from the heart. Don't be afraid to come close.'

'Afraid?'

'Yes. Because of the past, what happened to your family, you are wary about and wish to avoid being hurt, but I assure you that the last thing I want to do is to hurt or distress you in any way.'

'You seem to know me well, Laurence.'

'Well enough to deduce certain things. So what is it to be, Delphine? If I am to do all I want to do here at Pendene, then something must be established between us before I leave for London.'

His voice held a certain warmth and sincerity. Delphine was touched by it, yet she noted that he hadn't proposed to her with any show of affection and he did not mouth words of love he did not feel. However it was, she was going to take what had been offered, take it and hold it and keep it. She nodded, a little uncertainly. 'Very well. Yes, Laurence. I will marry you. I will be your wife.'

Relief shone in his eyes. 'There. That's settled

then. Now, I would like to show you Pendene—to let you see what you're in for. Would you like that?'

'Yes, I would love to see it.'

Side by side they sauntered back to the horses. A curious dreaminess pervaded Delphine as she let the sun's warmth seep into her. Time seemed to slow and everything around them was lulled in the shimmering heat. Tall grass and bracken grew everywhere and the merry chirrup of birds in the trees, the buzz of an occasional bee and the snorting of their horses were all that disturbed the quiet.

She looked at the high ground in the distance, remembering when she had been a child and her mother had delighted in riding with her through the countryside.

'What are you thinking?' Laurence asked. 'You have a wistful look on your face.'

'Have you ever been up on the moor?'

'No. You have?'

'Yes. My mother would take me there when I was little. She would let me run around to my heart's content, climbing rocks and jumping streams.'

'And you were happy.'

'I loved it, but it has another side to it—when the mind plays strange tricks the moment darkness comes. Some Cornish people have a natural horror of the moor after dark and have no desire to linger for longer than is necessary. It becomes a bleak and hostile landscape then, when the rocks become ghostly shapes. When the dark mist comes down, it can be misleading in which one can get hopelessly lost, even those who believe they know the moor. There's a gibbet there, where four lanes meet. It frequently encases a decaying body and the chains clank and creak as they move in the wind.'

'Some poor wretch who has fallen foul of the law.'

'Murderer, thief, highwayman or smuggler—what does it matter once they are dead? They hang there, carrion for the birds, and for the entire world to see—a sordid warning for those who choose to follow the same path. So have a care, Lord Beaumont, if you are serious about becoming a smuggler. You might well end up in the gibbet.'

He laughed at the very thought. 'Then should I be arrested for my crimes I will make a special request to be hung anywhere than on the moor.'

Delphine had ridden this way so often in the past that she knew when they were approaching Pendene. There was the tall gatehouse and between an avenue of tall trees stood Pendene itself. There was a beautiful house beneath the monstrous tangle of ivy and other creepers clinging to the walls and the entrance portico, the paint flaking from the casement windows and doors. All manner of vegetation filled the gardens and weeds sprouted from the cracks in the stone walls.

'Are you living here?' Delphine enquired, unable to believe they would be able to find their way into the house through the creepers.

'It may surprise you to know that, behind the overgrown façade, the house is habitable. The whole place needs money and more labour. It's my inheritance and I'm supposed to make it pay. It's inspired me and somehow I have to make it work.'

'I can see there is a lot of work to be done.'

'I came here as a child with my sisters. We loved it. When I arrived this time I felt some affection for the place. John McGuire and the labourers he hires when needed do a good job on the land, but the house has suffered—as you see. Come inside and I'll show you round.'

The door opened easily and they stepped inside. Delphine was pleased to see the interior hadn't suffered the ravages of the outside. With growing interest she began to look around. The honey-coloured oak-panelled hall was large with a carved oak staircase rising from the middle and family portraits littered the walls, reminding people that wealth had once been in the family. Through the open doors leading off from the hall she could see rooms with furniture covered over with protective sheets.

A woman appeared from somewhere, wiping her hands on her apron.

'Ah, this is Milly, Delphine. John McGuire's wife.'

Delphine smiled at the woman. 'Milly and I are already acquainted, Laurence. You can't live hereabouts without knowing all your neighbours. Hello, Milly. Forgive me if I appear surprised to find you here.'

'She's very kindly come to help out and, if we ask her nicely, she may get us a cup of tea—which, I expect, will have come from one of John's expeditions to Guernsey.'

Milly winked at Delphine. 'He's learning fast, this new Lord of the Manor.'

Delphine laughed. 'He'll have to if he is to live in Cornwall, Milly.' She looked at Laurence. 'It's a trade everyone in the county is linked to in one way or another.'

'I'll get you some tea—and it may run to a piece of cake.'

Milly disappeared to the domestic quarters and, taking her arm, Laurence escorted Delphine into a sitting room. The room had been made habitable and, despite the warm summer day outside, a fire was burning in the grate, giving the room a warm pleasant feeling.

'Well?' Laurence said, watching Delphine for her reaction to the house. 'What do you think? Will it do, do you think, for the new mistress of Pendene?'

Seating herself by the fire, Delphine smiled up at him. 'It will do very well—when she becomes its mistress. It does need a lot doing to it, but it's a lovely house.'

'When we've had tea I'll show you the rest of it. Thankfully it's been well preserved inside.'

'But it will still need money to be spent on it. Will the profit made from the estate cover it, do you think, or will you have to rely on your other source of income?'

'You mean if I decide to involve myself in the illicit trade of smuggling.' He shook his head with amusement. 'That is something I'm going to have to reconsider. The risks are too great—although it would enable me to live life rather better than the estate income will allow. Of course, if you do not approve of my other source of income, should I decide to become involved, then I will have no part in it.'

An impish smile tugged at Delphine's lips. 'Why should I object? I find the idea of being married to a smuggler rather romantic.'

He laughed. 'Now why does that not surprise me? I should tell you that when I return to London, I will take my plans for the mine with me, along with the experts' assessment of its potential, to negotiate with the banks to raise capital. I intended to do that in the first place had your grandfather refused to sell me the land, which, should I decide to become a smuggler, I would need to gain access to the cove to enable me to carry out my other…illicit activities.'

'Do you think the bank will agree to loan you the money?'

'I don't see why they shouldn't, but we'll have to see.'

Milly brought refreshments and, after they had finished drinking their tea, Laurence gave her a tour of the house. She loved it. Even though it had not been lived in for many years it had a welcome feel about it and she knew she would be content living there.

Later Laurence escorted her back to the cliff where they had met.

On the way back Delphine was a little silent and then she said, 'Laurence, I was wondering when you intend to see Grandfather. Milly has seen us together and people talk.'

'Now we've made our decision I'll call on him now if that is appropriate. The sooner the better. It's important that we get things sorted before I leave for London.'

'When?'

'Three weeks.' He looked at her. 'Time for us to be wed before I leave.'

She looked at him in a daze of confusion. He was already playing the role of her husband. He wanted to marry her, this she knew. He was charming and engaging and she thought that despite him telling her how some marriages were arranged with little thought to the feelings of the bride, she believed they could be happy. 'Oh—I—I hadn't thought...'

'Why not? Why wait? Time enough for the banns to be read and for us to be married before I have to leave.'

'How long do you expect to be gone?'

'A month—maybe longer. I promise you I will return just as soon as I sell the house and I have some money in the bank. Then I will be able to make plans. I know I have a lot to learn, but I'll soon get the hang of things.'

Reassured, Delphine fell silent, enjoying the beautiful scenery and warmed inside by the day's events. Was it possible that she could be beginning to look to the future with hope?

Delphine's grandfather was resting by the fire, a rug over his knees when they arrived at the house. She watched him turn his head expectantly when she entered the room and knew he would be rewarded to see she was accompanied by Laurence. When he made a feeble attempt to rise, she put her hand on his shoulder, pressing him back into the chair.

'Don't get up, Grandfather. There's no need to stand on ceremony.'

As they gave him the news that they had agreed to wed, he looked from one to the other.

'I will not pretend that this is not my dearest wish since I've made it blatantly obvious, but I hope, Delphine, that you've not agreed to do so because it is the wish of a dying man.'

To his astonishment, Delphine burst out laughing. 'Grandfather,' she said when she could speak calmly, 'I know you are not well, but will you please stop telling me you are a dying man. We all have to die some time. You are as cunning as a fox and I am sure could outwit the Devil himself.' Bending down, she gave him an affectionate kiss on the top of his head. 'Now aren't you going to wish us well—after all, you have got what you wanted.'

He cast a look at Laurence standing with his hands behind his back, amused by their interchange. 'You have agreed that you will marry?' he said.

'Yes, we have. I will take care of her. You have my word.'

'And you, Delphine?' He wanted to be convinced that this was what they both wanted. 'You are willing?'

Taking a deep breath, she nodded. The brutal fact was that without her grandfather and Aunt Amelia, without Laurence, she had no one in the world. Never had she wanted her father more than she did just then. 'Yes, I am willing.'

He nodded. 'I am entrusting my granddaughter into your keeping, Lord Beaumont, and I shall hold you personally responsible for her happiness, is that clear?'

'Quite clear,' Laurence answered in a solemn voice.

Jacob scrutinised his handsome, tranquil features sharply, then nodded. 'Good. As long as we understand one another. It goes without saying that her dowry will be generous—not in monetary terms—there's little in the bank but property.'

'What are you saying?' Delphine asked.

'The land—it will be part of your marriage settlement, along with the house, when I am gone. I have no one else to leave it to—and the war with France has taken away what should have come to you through your father.'

'We don't know that, Grandfather. There is no evidence that he has perished. I will keep on hoping he is alive somewhere in France.'

He nodded, touching her cheek gently. 'That is what I hope, too, Delphine. It is my dearest wish to see the two of you reunited. Will you marry soon?'

Delphine looked at Laurence for support.

'As soon as it can be arranged—as soon as the banns have been read. I have to return to London, so the sooner the better.'

'Will Delphine go with you?' Jacob asked, unable to conceal the note of alarm in his voice.

Knowing exactly what he was thinking, Delphine shook her head. His health was failing rapidly. Every day she saw a deterioration. She could not leave him. 'No. I will remain here in Cornwall. Laurence will return as soon as he has completed his business.'

Delphine stood aside as the two men fell into conversation. She took a moment to consider all that had happened that day, feeling that this had all happened very quickly, but then everything Laurence did seemed to take her by surprise. He spoke of a short engagement, but surely there must be more to a courtship, a period of mutual discovery and sweet anticipation? She wondered if she was giving in too quickly. Yet their kisses were too urgent to be contained for long. And by marrying Laurence, at least she and her grandfather would agree about her future.

Chapter Nine

While the banns were being read Laurence's time was taken up with getting to know his neighbours and learning as much as he could about the mine and its workings from those who knew everything there was to know about mining. He studied rock formations, air flow and drainage and anything else to be known about getting copper from the ground. When it was proven that there really was copper in the mine, Laurence was impatient to leave for London to settle matters there.

Delphine saw little of him. After the wedding it had been arranged that she would continue living with her grandfather until Laurence came back from London. They would then take up residence in their marital home. Milly McGuire was to remain at Pendene as housekeeper, and Laurence had asked her to employ staff to make the house habitable for when they moved in.

After a busy day climbing up and down ladders at the mine and discussing plans with the experts, Laurence decided to head to the cove for a swim. He rode to the cliff edge and tethered his horse behind a group of trees before making his way down to the beach. He branched off towards the hidden cove. The sea was deep blue and calm, with prisms of light dancing on the surface and just enough movement for the waves to break gently on the sand.

His mother had encouraged him and his siblings to swim when they had come down to Cornwall, telling them that the exercise and salt water was good for them. Now Laurence stripped off his clothes, except for his white breeches rolled up to the knee, headed for a rock pool and plunged into the water.

It was an exhilarating feeling as the blessed coolness enveloped him, caressing his skin like silk. He was a strong, vigorous swimmer and he cleaved the water with long flowing strokes, careful to keep within the confines of the cove so as not to be seen from the headland. Having swum far enough, he returned more slowly to the shore.

Before he reached it he realised he wasn't the only swimmer to make use of the cove. Treading water, he watched as a young woman sauntered unhurriedly along what she thought to be a deserted beach. When she removed her broad-brimmed hat and her golden hair was exposed to the sun, his lips broke into a slow smile on recognising Delphine. She clearly hadn't seen his clothes beside the rocks as she began removing her clothes to allow herself more freedom.

In just a flimsy undergarment that barely reached her knees, she waded into the shallows before plunging forward in a gentle arc, immersing her entire body, the slight swell billowing out her loose garment. She swam beneath the surface and after a few moments broke through. Swimming out to the mouth of the cove with strong, sure strokes, she paused and floated on her back, her face upturned to the sun, her hair floating about her head.

Laurence could have swum to shore and slipped away up the path while she was away from the beach, but he was so entranced by her that he just stayed where he was.

Moving effortlessly through the water, pausing now and then to float on her back, it was during one of these periods of respite that Delphine became aware of a soft, regular splashing close by of someone swimming. Rearing up out of the water just in time to see someone swimming fast and powerfully towards her, cutting the water and disappearing from sight, in sudden panic she trod water, looking around frantically for the swimmer to surface.

To her horror a hard arm threaded around her waist, jerking her back against a hard chest. She opened her mouth to scream, almost swallowing a mouthful of sea water, when mercifully her assailant lifted her up and she heard him laugh.

At first she was amazed, then outraged. 'Laurence!' she gasped, indignant. 'What are you doing? I would have thought you'd have enough to do at Pendene without coming here to swim. How long have you been watching me?'

A slow appreciative smile touched his lips. 'Long enough.' His smouldering gaze passed over her face. 'Long enough to realise you swim like a fish.' His arm was still holding her waist. Time was suspended as, trying to ignore her mixed emotions, Delphine stared at him. A lazy, devastating grin swept across his face. 'Like you I was drawn to the cove for a swim.'

'I love to swim. I'm fortunate to live by the sea in order to do so.'

'I know of no other woman who would want to.'

'I must look a sight. No doubt after this you'll probably change your mind about marrying me.' As she said this she was unaware that her golden hair, soaked and clinging to her head, was many different shades and dazzling lights. Laurence's expression was unreadable, smiling, watchful, a knowing look in his eyes. *What kind of man are you, Laurence Beaumont?* she wondered, and realised she had no idea at all. She gave him a speculative look, deeply conscious that his calm exterior hid the inner man.

'There's no danger of that,' he told her.

Brought abruptly from her ponderous thoughts, she let out a startled shriek as his hands again lifted her up out of the water playfully. 'That,' she cried with laughing severity as Laurence raked his wet hair back and grinned at her, 'was a very silly and childish thing to do. Almost as childish as this,' she said, sliding her hand over the surface of the water and sending a spray of water into his face before ducking for cover under the water to avoid reprisal and beginning to swim towards shallow water.

Unfortunately she didn't get far before a laughing, carefree ducking and fooling about followed that left Delphine exhausted and heading for shore with Laurence close behind. Padding up the beach, she flopped down on to her back, her chest heaving from her exertions, her legs stretched out in front of her.

'You play too rough,' she reprimanded good-naturedly. 'I'm safer here on the beach.'

Hands on hips, Laurence stood looking down at her, dripping water, and quietly, he said, 'I would be as gentle as you wish me to be, Delphine.'

Delphine melted inside at the meaning she read in his words. Half opening her eyes, she squinted up at him. Through the veil of her eyelashes she could see the rugged planes of his face. The breath froze in her throat. His only article of clothing was his white sodden breeches, rolled up over his muscular calves.

He was well over six feet of splendid masculinity, firmly muscled and broad shouldered and narrow hipped. His chest was covered with a furring of black hair that narrowed as it reached his flat abdomen and dipped below the waistband of his breeches. Disconcerted and embarrassed by the way the sight of his shining body was affecting her, she closed her eyes.

He sat beside her, bending his knee on which he rested his arm. 'Your clothes are wet,' he remarked, a slow grin spreading across his lips. He seemed casually unconcerned with his state of undress.

'They usually are when one's been swimming,' she replied, her tone slightly sarcastic. 'It doesn't matter. They'll soon dry in this heat.'

'You are quite shameless—do you know that?'

'I don't care. We are to be married, so it doesn't really matter that you see me in a state of dishabille, does it?'

'If you say so. I'm not prepared to argue with you in case you decide to put your clothes on.'

Delphine was excruciatingly aware of his eyes on her as he gazed at her for a long moment, sweeping down the length of her and back again. She abruptly realised how very alone they were, but she made no attempt to reach for her clothes and cover herself. She squinted up at him. 'Don't you have things to do at Pendene?'

'I'll have you know I've put in a full day at the mine, climbing up and down ladders and trying to learn as much as I can until my head's fit to burst. Besides, I'd much rather be here with you.'

'Trying to seduce me, you mean. And you call me shameless.'

He trailed his fingers lightly down her bare upper arm. Her face, young, vulnerable and defenceless and turning a lovely golden colour, was naked beneath the heavy crop of her hair.

Sitting up, she tossed back her hair with a flick of her head, splattering them both with droplets of sea water. Laurence got to his feet and stepped back. Her soaked bodice clung to her body, outlining the shapely peaks of her breasts that were high and firm, fuller than her wraith-like slenderness indicated. Seeing where his gaze was directed, Delphine felt indecently exposed.

'Must you look at me like that?'

'It's hard when I know I should turn my eyes away.'

Delphine could feel herself responding to his closeness and the softness of his voice. Maybe it was an indefinable impression, an illusion, a trick of the sun's bright light reflecting off the water, but he seemed changed somehow. What was it? What was in the turn of his lips as though he smiled at some private thought? She was gazing up at him strangely, too, assessing him in some way, her gaze reflective, a glow of something in her eyes, which were a soft amber velvet.

Getting to her feet, she brushed the sand off her body and began walking up the beach to where she had left her clothes. Closer to the shadow of the overhanging rocks the air hung motionless. There was a strange silence in the cove. Laurence had followed her. His eyes met hers in the shadowy light.

'You're not afraid of being here alone with me, are you, Delphine?'

'No, of course not,' she answered, struggling for the last vestige of her thin control, feeling it crack under the strain as he studied her, and her initial feeling of embarrassment was replaced almost at once with sheer delight as he trailed a fingertip over her shoulder and down her upper arm. 'Since we are to be married, it is something I'll have to get used to.'

He moved closer, his eyes looking at her for a long moment, and Delphine had the strange sensation of falling. Her heartbeat quickened. She breathed deeply, disturbingly affected by his nearness. Droplets of water still clung to his skin and tinier beads sparkled in the dark furring of his chest. His hair was a dark halo in the light, and his gaze was fixed deliberately on her—assessing, lingering and seducing.

His smile broadened as his eyes searched her face, then his smile faded and he grew serious. She looked away and colour warmed her cheeks. He was devouring her with his eyes. There was a fire in the green depths, a blaze of passion and remembrance of the kisses they had shared before, and longing. A longing that she knew she was feeling, too.

'All I can think of is that, in a few short days, you will be my wife.'

His rich voice trapped her in a web of sensual anticipation. 'Yes—yes, I will.'

His eyes were in shadow, but they seemed to glow. Gently taking her upper arms, he drew her to his naked chest and slowly lowered his mouth to hers. Having thought of little else since they had kissed at the mine, it was beyond her power to deny them both another taste of the pleasure it had given them. She could not resist him any more than the treacherous melting feeling that was stealing over her. Her body grew liquid and she wanted the sensual assault of his kisses, his caress.

As she had grown she had noted the physical changes in her body, but the emotional changes that were supposed to come along with that had somehow eluded her. Perhaps that was because the years of her development to maturity had been taken up with the grief she had felt at the loss of her family, her work to secure the safety of those fleeing France and her desperation to find her father.

Since meeting Laurence she had experienced feelings within her body associated with sexual matters and ever since he had kissed her a natural curiosity to know more had stirred inside her, a curiosity she wanted to assuage. The kiss had kindled her senses, unleashing a passion in her that she'd never experienced before. There was a fire in her veins, sensual and pagan, and for the first time in her life she felt restless with excitement. She couldn't trust herself to be close to him, when her whole body was alive with sensation.

Turning her face up to his, Laurence took what she offered and claimed her lips in hungry greed, while his fingers glided over her back. Her body trembled as his hand slowly crept up her belly and cupped her breast while not releasing her lips. He squeezed her nipple between his thumb and finger so that her breasts seemed to grow heavier, fuller, giving her such beguiling pleasure. She quivered and let out a restless moan.

With the rhythm of his fingertips caressing her breast, her body reacted of its own accord. Arching her back, she thrust her breast more fully into his large, warm palm. Slowly they went down on their knees, their lips still joined together. His kiss deepened, his mouth only leaving her lips to travel down her chin, her neck and down the valley between her breasts. Overwhelmed by his passion, she lay down on the sand. The sea air and the heat of the sand she found extremely exciting.

Laurence lay beside her and she ran her fingers through his dark hair as he lightly trailed skilled fingers down her neck. She gasped, a warmth suffusing her cheeks. Though she commanded herself to move, her body refused to budge. She felt it so strongly, it was as if her whole body was throbbing suddenly and in her head her thoughts were not orderly—just odd, strong responses. And in her breasts—how could a touch, a caress, reach her breasts? Yet it had—it was making them desperate to be touched again and it was all she could do not to reach for one of his hands and place it there.

And the sensation moved on, lower, sweetly soft and liquid—small darts of pleasure travelled as if on silken threads to her stomach and inner thighs as he continued his rhythmic stroking. The heat of his hand seemed to scorch her cool flesh as it ventured lower and she licked her dry lips.

'I think you overstep yourself, Laurence,' she murmured, a little breathless while not moving away despite her remark.

'But you enjoy me touching you, Delphine, do you not?' Laurence muttered in a tight, strained voice. 'Would you deny either of us the pleasures of being together?'

'How on earth could I do that when I'm lying near naked in your arms?'

He found her lips once more. She felt devoured by his kiss. His voice was low and husky in her ears as his lips trailed to her ears and whispered endearments, and she had to reach deeply into her reservoir of will to dispel the slow numbing of her senses. A hunger was growing inside her, a hunger that only he could satisfy.

Facing each other on their sides, Delphine pulled away. When he would have drawn her back she stopped him. 'Please don't think I make a habit of making free with my affections. What I am saying is that what I have done with you is something I would not do with anyone else. I know nothing about the physical side of marriage and had nobody to ask. I always thought that when it happened I would rely on my instincts.'

Laurence took her hand in a gesture of understanding. 'What are you trying to say, Delphine?'

'I'm not telling you this to gain your sympathy. What I'm saying is that you are different to anyone I have ever known. I'm not sure how I should feel or what it is that I want. What I do know is that I'm glad we're going to be married.' She paused and Laurence glanced at her. She saw his glance and blushed. 'I have shown myself to you as someone who cares about you—I have even shown myself to you half-naked,' she said, her blush deepening, 'and I care about what you think.'

'Delphine, you are the most beautiful person that I have ever seen. I feel privileged that you have shown yourself to me and that you are to be my wife—and the sooner the better. I shall try to restrain myself, difficult as that will be over the coming days.'

She looked at him steadily, their faces so close their breath mingled. 'Do you have to do that? Do we have to wait? Will you not make love to me now?' To end it now would leave her feeling incomplete, cheated somehow, empty and aching for what only he could give her. She didn't want that. She couldn't allow that.

'Please, Laurence,' she whispered, planting tiny kisses at the corner of his mouth. 'You are going away after the wedding—for how long I dread to think. I am going to miss you dreadfully. Why can we not enjoy each other now?'

'Would you not prefer a soft bed for your first experience?'

'No. This is where I would like it to be—with the sea's waves breaking on the sand. Then every time I come to the cove I will remember.'

Tightening his arm about her waist, he slowly lowered his mouth to hers and kissed her gently. Delphine closed her eyes and slipped her arms around his neck. 'You'll have to show me how it's done,' she whispered against his lips. 'I've had no practice, you see, so I would not know.'

'I will teach you. I will waken all the passion in your lovely, untutored body. Are you ready to learn?'

His half-smile was so seductive it sent a thrill all the way down Delphine's body. 'Do you make a habit of deflowering virgins?'

'Not usually.'

'Would you like to see more of me—before we…?'

The slow smile spreading across his lips told her he would.

Quickly she wriggled out of her remaining protection while he slipped out of his breeches. Proud, savage and determined, his splendid form gleamed in the soft light.

Side by side on the sand Delphine's flesh burned as she felt Laurence's eyes caress her, tease her, and she shivered and drew in her breath in a half-startled gasp when his strong fingers gently explored every inch of her, cupping, touching, tracing the line of her waist and over the curve of her hips with sure mastery of his subject. Slowly she allowed her own gaze to stray over the contours of his godlike body stretched out beside her, from his shoulders and deep chest, to the muscles of his arms and down to his tender fingers.

By now all rational thought had flown from her head. With an abandon that shocked her, she melted against him, the glorious mass of her hair resting on him like a golden coverlet as her senses clamoured for him to possess her. Responding to the need he was so skilful at building in her, yielding to the exquisite pleasure of his touch, she realised that Laurence Beaumont was a man of extraordinary skill and power as he rolled her on to her back.

Suddenly his weight was on her, and the desire burning in those green eyes looking down at her was like a savage force. Kissing her with a raw, urgent hunger, he slipped his knee between her thighs and slowly he entered her, filling her, until suddenly she felt a stab of pain.

Feeling her body jerk and hearing the soft cry she tried to muffle in his shoulder, Laurence paused and stared down at her. 'Sweet God in heaven! I hurt you.'

'It's all right—truly,' she whispered against his cheek. 'Don't stop now.'

When he began to move inside her that was the moment Delphine ceased to think. Something began to uncoil in the pit of her stomach, which gathered momentum with each deep thrust. His hands were beneath her, moulding her hips to take her deeper, and her flesh clutched in spasms at his invading force, sending lust to the point of total surrender. The shooting darts of bliss penetrating the depths of her belly loosened her joints so that her arms encircling his shoulders went limp. She arched her back, the soft globes of her breasts pressed flat against his chest. Entwined, they merged together, fulfilling each other in a most sublime act of love, Delphine's firm, slender body on fire as she gave all her desire and her passion.

Wave after wave of exquisite torture washed over her and only Laurence's steadying rhythm kept her from journeying beyond herself. Exulting silently, she felt herself being ruled by him, possessed by him, feeling his need burning through her with infinite power, igniting her female flesh with new life. They were wrapped in the pure rapture of their union, with no quarter given as senses were besieged, man and woman as close as it was possible to be, yielding and merging with each other.

And then it was over, the explosion of pleasure engulfing everything. Reluctant to draw apart, they lay together. Delphine had no immediate thoughts, only the memory of something immense, something important, of incredible joy, tremendous and wondrous, beyond which nothing was comparable. The man who had brought her to such heights of incredible bliss, this man to whom she had given herself, had become her lover in every sense of the word. He had made her into a woman, had given her true knowledge of herself and she was glad it had been him.

It seemed a long time before Laurence stirred and shifted to his side, drawing her close as they listened to the gentle sloughing of the sea as it broke on the sand. Gazing at the incredibly lovely young woman nestling in the crook of his arm, her satiated body aglow from the force of her passion, he felt strangely humble and possessive. For a while she had held him spellbound as life and passion had seemed to sing in her body.

The enchanting temptress who had yielded to him without reservation, who had writhed beneath him, had been vibrant and alive in his arms. After so long an abstinence he had felt his own body grow hot and hard with a desire to possess her. He had wanted her with an intensity that was painful and he had been unable to think of anything else and, when he had buried himself in her sweet warmth, everything before and what was to come after was swept away. Tenderly, he stroked her arm, trying not to think and to hold on to the fading euphoria.

'I'm sorry if I hurt you. Are you all right?'

Rolling on to her stomach, leaning on his chest, she placed small kisses on his chin. 'Yes. It hurt a little,' she murmured. 'Only at first. After that the pain went away.' She sighed. 'Thank you, Laurence.'

'For what?'

'Making love to me.'

'It was my pleasure,' he replied, tucking a thick strand of tangled hair behind her ear. 'Although I'm beginning to think I should have left the beach while I had the chance.' Suddenly she giggled. 'What amuses you?'

'I can't believe I've done this incredible, wanton thing and let you make love to me without a stitch on and without a ring on my finger.'

'I'm impatient to make you my wife. I want to be the one to protect you, the one you will turn to for comfort and loving. To have you in my bed and in my arms.'

Delphine laughed lightly. 'So you want to claim ownership of me. I will be your wife—your equal, on terms that are agreeable to us both—but I will not be owned. But I do want your love, Laurence, more than anything.'

'Then you have it,' he whispered. 'All of it.'

Satisfied, she nestled closer to him. 'I feel rather like some kind of wanton. Do you think it was wicked of me to give myself to you like that?'

Laurence chuckled low in his chest. 'Wicked? As to that I shall have to give it some thought. If sexual pleasure is classed as wicked, then I am impatient for the next time. But you are not wicked, Delphine. You haven't a wicked bone in your body. But you have much to learn and I will enjoy teaching you so that your body will become an instrument of pleasure. I will make it sing, Delphine. Do you regret what we did—pre-empting our wedding vows?'

'No. I've had a taste of the forbidden sweetness, which was both intoxicating and exquisite. I shall look forward to being your wife, Laurence. But now I think I'd better put my clothes on and get back. Grandfather worries if I'm gone too long.'

Reluctantly he released her. Getting to their feet, they pulled on their clothes. Delphine wrinkled her nose.

'What is it? Is something wrong?'

'My clothes are full of sand and it's most unpleasant next to my skin. But not to worry. I'll have a bath and wash it away when I get back to the house.'

'Me, too—when I arrive at Pendene.'

With Laurence's arm draped about Delphine's waist, together they walked across the sand and up the incline to the top of the cliff, where Laurence collected his horse. Taking Delphine in his arms, he held her close before releasing her.

'Take care, Delphine. I'll try to see you before the wedding. If not, I'll see you in the church.'

The day of the wedding arrived and the sun shone with golden promise. The ceremony was to take place at ten o'clock at the local church. Laurence was to leave for London as soon as it was over, putting their wedding night on hold until his return.

Beset by pre-wedding nerves, which Agatha told her affected most young women on their wedding day, not for the first time Delphine asked herself if she was sure that she was doing the right thing and consoled herself with the conviction that Laurence did actually care for her. She replayed their time together on the beach over and over in her mind. The mere thought of what she had done brought a scarlet flush to her cheeks. Perhaps she should not have given in so easily, she thought while cooling her warm cheeks.

There was something primitively male about him that made her tremble at the thought of him making love to her again. Those sharp green eyes that seemed to see right through her defences, sensing her surrender before she had realised it herself. And that wicked little scar on his eyelid added to the illusion of savagery.

Her grandfather was too poorly to attend the wedding, as was Aunt Amelia, who had taken to her bed following a fall, but she had sent Delphine her love and best wishes and told her she would consider travelling to Tregannon before too long. Delphine was concerned about her and decided she would ride into Fowey to see her when Laurence had left for London. Expressing her concern to her grandfather, after a moment of thoughtful silence, for the first time in years he spoke fondly of his sister, saying he would write a letter to her which Delphine could take with her.

There were only a few present at the wedding, which was conducted on a balmy morning in the nearby village. There had been no family at Pendene for fifteen years or more, but the church had retained a couple of family pews in the church. Word had quickly spread that the new Lord of the Manor had arrived to take up residence and was to wed Delphine, so some of the villagers had turned out to stand in the street to witness the event.

A vision of loveliness in a dress of cream silk and as slender as a wand, her hair unbound, clutching a small bouquet of late summer flowers, Delphine arrived at the church with John McGuire, who was standing in for her grandfather. With her heart in her throat Delphine entered the little church.

There was a special radiance inside. Last-minute fears surged within her like fluttering birds as she contemplated all the unknowns of her future with Laurence Beaumont, but on seeing him waiting for her at the altar, tall and powerful, looking extremely handsome in his fine clothes, his dark hair brushed smoothly back and secured at his nape, she couldn't take her eyes off him. Casting the last of her fears aside, she walked to stand by his side to repeat the solemn, binding vows.

As the vicar intoned the final words that joined them in holy matrimony, Laurence turned towards her. Taking her hands, he drew her close, placing his lips on hers to seal their vows.

When it came to the signing of the register, Laurence casually looked at their written names. His brow creased into a frown when he saw Delphine's name—Delphine St Clair.

'St Clair?' he queried, continuing to stare down at

the name. It was as if a ghost had suddenly entered the church.

Delphine looked at him. 'Of course. I'm sorry, Laurence. I should have told you but—I just didn't think. My mother was an Arlington until she married my father.'

Laurence's face tightened and he was looking at her most oddly, his expression bemused. 'What was his name?'

'Henri—Henri St Clair. Why—is it important?'

He laughed softly, uneasily. 'No—no, of course not. Now come, I have time to enjoy some of our wedding breakfast before I have to leave for London.'

They went to Tregannon for the small wedding breakfast, to which a few close neighbours were invited, and the atmosphere was light-hearted. But despite his pleasant manner and never letting her out of his sight for a moment, Delphine sensed a subtle change in Laurence. Perhaps it was his new status as a husband that had brought about the change, or that he was to leave her and he was sorry for it, but her instinct told her it was something else.

'Marriage obviously agrees with you,' Laurence told her softly when he managed to get her to himself. 'I have never seen you look more delectable as you do at this moment.'

'Don't all brides?' she murmured.

'I only have eyes for the one,' he replied. 'Lady Beaumont.'

She laughed happily. 'I have hardly given that a thought. I never thought this would happen to me.

Can you imagine it? Me! Lady Beaumont. Oh—I'll never get used to it.'

'Yes, you will.' He looked at her, his wonderful bright green eyes warm and full of affection, and he smiled a smile that would melt any woman's heart. 'I'm sorry I'm leaving you so soon, Delphine. Hopefully I'll be back very soon and we can begin our lives as husband and wife.'

And then it was time for him to go, the coach and the driver who had brought him to Pendene waiting to take him back to London. But not for long, he assured her. They would be together again soon.

Delphine followed him to the coach. He grasped her shoulders lightly and gazed into her eyes. 'I hate leaving you. Look after yourself, my darling wife. Everything will be different when I return.'

Without a word, Delphine reached for him. He pulled her close and hugged her. They held each other for a long moment in silence and then he released her. Without another word he climbed into the coach and she stood and watched it on its way before going back inside.

The unease she had felt on signing the register in the church had not left her. She could not put her finger on it, but something was not quite right. Looking back on the day, she recalled the moment Laurence had changed. It was when he had seen her maiden name—St Clair. There had been something distant in his whole attitude and when he had looked at her there had been a dazed confusion in his gaze.

He'd recognised the name—it had meant something to him. But why? How? And then a thought so profound, so shocking—that the name was familiar to him because he knew her father—hit her with a lightning force.

If her suspicion was correct, why had he kept it from her? Drowning in a black pool of despair, mechanically she stepped outside, her arms wrapped round her waist in an agony of suffering, staring blankly at the drive down which Laurence's coach had disappeared. Feeling sick to her stomach, she tried to collect her wits. What on earth should she do? She wanted to go after him, to demand he tell her what he knew, but he had gone on his way, taking the truth with him.

It was a deeply troubled man who left Tregannon. When Laurence had seen Delphine's maiden name written down, he couldn't believe what he was seeing. The name, St Clair, brought unspeakable memories into his brain, causing his head to spin, thoughts chasing themselves in circles as he searched for a way out of this without hurting Delphine, without breaking her heart on her wedding day, a day that was meant to be the happiest day of her life.

Why had he not thought to ask—not that it would have made any difference for he would have married her anyway. But her name—the name of her father, the man she believed was still alive—he knew. Had he not spent time with him in the Conciergerie, but whereas for him there had been freedom and hope, for Henri St Clair there was continued incarceration until the day he would be taken before the tribunal and, like the rest of his family before him, sent to the guillotine.

The name conjured up the year he had spent as a prisoner and in his imagination he relived, slowly, every minute he had been deprived of his freedom, believing there was only one way out—death. Before he told Delphine that he knew her father, he would make enquiries at the Foreign Office, see if there was some way he could discover what had happened to Henri St Clair, and if he was still in the Conciergerie, before facing Delphine with what he knew.

The day after her wedding Delphine rode into Fowey to visit her aunt, taking with her a letter from her grandfather. Entering the house and not finding her aunt in her chair by the hearth, she went up the stairs. She had a premonition. In her heart she knew something was wrong. Her aunt was lying in bed as if asleep, but Delphine could see from the waxen look on her face that she was dead. Her heart wrenched with sorrow and tears trailed down her cheeks. Her thoughts turned to her grandfather, of how he would feel and react to the death of his sister.

After tending her aunt's body and arranging to have her taken to Tregannon, she left Fowey to break the news to her grandfather. During the ride back to Tregannon she felt nothing, but the hour which had lapsed had brought a sense of unreality to her. In her grandfather's room she faced him, going to sit on the bed and taking his hand in hers. He looked at her, at the anguish she was unable to hide on her face, and he knew.

Closing his eyes, he seemed to melt into the pillows propping up his frail body, his hand tightening on Delphine's before releasing it. His face was a mirror of her own desolation. She didn't know what to say, what to think.

'So,' he said softly, 'Amelia is gone. I was too late—too late to make amends, fool that I am. It serves me right.'

Not forty-eight hours after the death of his sister, her grandfather passed on.

Delphine often wondered how she got through the following days, for her emotions were in turmoil and her spirit low. The days were overshadowed in her memory. She was aware of doing and saying the things she had to in preparation of burying what might be her two remaining relatives if it was found that her father was dead, also. Following the most unbearable tragedies when night and day seemed to merge into one, there was no peace for Delphine. She struggled during the times she was alone to hold back her cries of anguish, but at times they broke through and she would weep tears of profound grief.

She had known her grandfather would leave her one day, but now that day had come she was brokenhearted at his passing. She left the house and walked in the woods, wandering along paths and through flower-filled pastures, where birds warbled merrily and bees and butterflies flitted from one glorious bloom to another, settling and drowsily moving in the fragile warmth. Eventually she found her way to the cliff and stared out to sea as the sun set in a purple haze and in her mind she was back at her mother's side and with her aunt and uncle in France.

It was strange that she should feel this way, that she could feel their arms reaching out to her, yet they were gone and, much as she wanted them, in reality she was alone. But not alone—not entirely. She had Laurence. A warmth began creeping into her heart, a warmth and a need to have his arms around her, to comfort her and love her.

But there was also unease and a feeling of betrayal when she recalled their parting and that her instinct told her he was keeping information concerning her father from her. But then again she could be wrong. Was she so desperate for news of her father that she was prepared to grasp at anything she thought might lead her to him?

That was when she decided to take the post and travel to London.

Chapter Ten

Laurence entered the hallowed halls of White's, the gentleman's club in St James's. The rooms were cloaked in the quiet, restrained ambience, redolent of the masculine smells of sandalwood, leather and cigars. He was there to meet with Sir Godfrey Bucklow. They sat surrounded by ornately carved mahogany furniture. The atmosphere was heavy, the aroma of tobacco lingering in the air. They were seated in Sir Godfrey's favourite corner, where he always sat to savour his port and read his newspaper and indulge in conversation with his companions.

They had discussed at length the troubles in America and the politics of the day and now they turned their attention to the troubles in France. After politely enquiring about the health of Delphine, Sir Godfrey sat back and prepared to discuss the reason for their meeting.

'I have known Delphine and the Arlington family all my life—are we not neighbours? I look forward to having you as a neighbour now you are to take up residence at Pendene and Delphine, as your wife, will be happy there, I know it. She is a remarkable young woman—resilient and enduringly devoted to those she cares about. She's a highly intelligent young lady with a certain wilfulness about her—a certain head-strong quality which I admire. But then, I don't have to tell you that. You are a lucky man.'

'I agree with you. She is quite extraordinary.'

'When her father's side of the family was killed, she approached me with her offer to help people escape France. I didn't expect her to be so successful. I didn't want to involve her, knowing how her grand-father would have forbidden it, but she was adamant. She is convinced her father is still alive—although any chance of that I always thought was a remote one until you told me you have seen him.'

'I have—and spoken to him in the Conciergerie. I had no idea he was Delphine's father until the wed-ding ceremony. That was when I realised who she was. As far as I know Henri St Clair is still there. Un-fortunately his health was not good and he had lost a lot of weight. God willing, he is still alive. After my spell in the Conciergerie I decided not to return to France, to retire from my work with the Intelligence Service, but I would like to do one last task to try to get him out. I have to do this for Delphine, Sir God-frey—I am sure you will understand.'

'Of course I do. I will make enquiries from other agents who have recently returned from France. If he went to the guillotine, someone will know. If not, then we can assume he is still in that infernal prison. What will you tell Delphine?'

'Nothing. I don't want to build up her hopes, only to have them come crashing down should I fail in my mission to get him out and bring him safely to England.'

'You would go over there—after what happened to you?'

'Yes, I will. I have to.'

'Then leave it with me. I will arrange everything. If he is indeed still alive then we will find a way to get him out.'

By the time Delphine arrived in London, three days after leaving Cornwall, trying to keep her aching loss at bay, her patience was close to breaking point as she suffered the aggravating slowness of the coach's progress. It had never entered her head to ask Laurence his London address—fortunately John McGuire gave it to her. From the coaching inn she hired a coach to take her to Mayfair, giving the driver the address.

The London roads were congested with all manner of vehicles and people. It seemed to take an age to reach Mayfair and when the coach finally pulled up outside an impressive, elegant town house with a pale stone exterior and steps leading up to a shiny, black-painted door, she breathed a sigh of relief. The driver deposited her bag next to her and left her to await the door being opened to admit her.

It was opened by a silver-haired butler. He looked her up and down before saying, 'Yes?'

'This is Lord Beaumont's residence?'

'It is.'

'Oh, that's a relief. Is he at home?'

'Who is asking?'

'His wife.'

Brows that were as silver as his hair rose up his forehead and his eyes widened in disbelief. 'His wife? Forgive me, but I did not know that Lord Beaumont had a wife.'

'Well, now you do.' Delphine raised her chin to a lofty angle. She might look rumpled and travel-stained and had arrived without a maid in attendance, but she did know how things were done as the daughter of a French count and she could feign a conceited self-worth when necessary. 'So are you going to let me in or must I remain in the street until you have informed my husband of my arrival?'

He looked at her with the sharp eyes of a seasoned soldier. He clearly sensed she was telling the truth. 'Do forgive me. Please, step inside, Lady Beaumont.'

The interior of the house was a lavish display of wealth. The large staircase led to a landing which boasted marble pillars and beautiful Grecian statues in niches. It was a perfect place for the family to greet their guests in grand style. Having been raised in a similar fashion, Delphine was used to such grandeur so she wasn't overwhelmed by it, but knowing of Laurence's reduced circumstances, she was surprised by it.

'So, is my husband at home?' she asked, a smile curving her lips, the kind of smile she used to charm and disarm in order to get her way.

'I'm afraid not. I believe he's at his club in St James's, my lady.'

'Then if you will have someone show me to a room where I can wait—or better still a bedchamber—and have my bags brought up. I would like to freshen up. I've travelled up from Cornwall and I would appreciate a bath if you can have water sent up.'

'You—you have a maid?' he said, not having closed the door and expecting a maid to materialise at any moment.'

'I don't have one.'

'Then I'll arrange for one of the maids to attend you—although the staff have been thinned out of late...'

'I quite understand,' she said softly. 'I can tend to myself. I'm used to doing so.'

It was midnight when Laurence arrived home. From where she was sitting in the drawing room, Delphine watched him walk vigorously into the room and cross to the sideboard and pour himself a brandy. The glass was halfway to his lips when, on raising his eyes and glancing in the mirror in front of him, his hand froze on seeing a figure sitting silently in the chair across the room, watching him intently.

'Good Lord!' he said, spinning round, splashing the brandy down his suit. 'Delphine!' Placing the glass on the tray, he strode across the room towards her. 'What are you doing here? Why didn't you write and tell me you were coming?'

'Hello, Laurence. There wasn't time. I left Cornwall in rather a hurry.'

'Your grandfather?'

'He died—so has my aunt. They are both gone. Naturally my first thought was to come to London to find my husband.' He reached out a hand to her, but stilled on meeting her hard gaze. 'Aunt Amelia died the day after we were married. My grandfather the day after that. They never did resolve their differences. Grandfather wrote her a letter, but it was too late. They loved each other really. It was just a stupid disagreement that kept them apart—and too much pride. They were both old and had so much to give each other towards the end, but they were both stubborn and refused to give an inch.'

'You're still in shock, I can sense that. To lose the two people you were so close to—for them to die like that—good Lord, Delphine, I'm sorry. That is what has brought you to London?'

'That—and another matter.'

'Oh? And what is that?'

Steeling herself for what was to come, then getting to her feet, she stepped away from him while keeping her eyes fixed on his. 'It's about honesty, openness and trust. Stupidly I thought we had agreed to that in our marriage.'

He raised a questioning brow. 'We did?'

'It has to have been somewhere in our marriage vows. I now find I have got it so very wrong. How can I trust you when you are up to your eyes in deception?'

'Deception? What the hell are you talking about?' His voice was icy.

'My father.' She met him look for look and her eyes were cold. 'I want the truth about what you know.'

For a moment his face took on an expression of total incomprehension. He frowned as though he were doing his best to unravel her words, to make sense of them, then his face hardened when realisation of what she was saying hit him. 'Your father...?' His voice died away and he turned from her, as if he couldn't bear to look at her. 'Your father? What about your father?'

Delphine knew she must seem odd. How could she help it when the words she wanted to speak— shout—at him were roiling at the back of her throat in an effort to get out? 'You tell me, Laurence, and don't pretend you don't know what I'm talking about. Do you know him?' she asked, enunciating each word slowly. 'Have you seen him? If so, you had better tell me.'

He turned back to her, his face devoid of all expression. 'How did you know?'

'I remember how you reacted when you saw my maiden name in the church. It was not unknown to you, was it? You had seen or heard it before, hadn't you?'

'Then, yes, Delphine. I have seen him.'

She moved a little closer to him, her hands clenched by her sides. He was watching her warily, having schooled himself well in the necessity for restraint in trying circumstances like the one he now faced. 'Where, Laurence? Where have you seen him?'

He moved to stand in front of her rigid figure,

where he stood looking down at her upturned face. She glared at him with a mix of fury and pain. His face became tense. 'In the Conciergerie.'

The word seemed to hang in the air between them. A tremor of horror rippled through her and, with a sudden spurt of anger, she repeated, 'The Conciergerie. I cannot believe you would do this to me. You know how important this is to me. You know I have been searching for information of my father ever since my aunt and uncle went to the guillotine—putting myself in danger constantly in my desperation to find him. You knew what it meant to me—and—and yet you do this. How could you? I have every right to be angry. When did you see him? When?'

'At the beginning of my own incarceration—but I didn't know he was your father at the time. I knew him as Henri St Clair—a French nobleman awaiting execution. He was ill and was moved to another cell. I was not aware of the connection between the two of you until the day of our marriage.'

'So, I was right in my suspicion. You knew—you saw him?' she asked in a small voice, incredulous.

Laurence pushed his hand through his thick hair, his eyes darkening. 'Yes, Delphine, I saw him. I even spoke to him on occasion, but we were not kept together so I was given no insight into his past.'

For a second Delphine thought she was going mad. There was a red mist before her eyes and a storm of utter fury in her heart such as she had never felt before. 'And—and you weren't going to tell me? Have you any idea how much that hurts me? I have a right to know. Is—is he alive?' she asked, her eyes wide and anxious, wanting to know, yet dreading what he would say.

'As to that I cannot tell you.' He sighed, putting his hand on her arm to draw her close. 'I understand that you are upset…'

'I am not upset. I am furious. You have deceived me most cruelly,' she uttered with a rage that was buried bone deep. Shaking his hand off her arm, she stepped away from him, as if she couldn't bear to be near him.

'Forgive me for deceiving you. I was genuinely concerned how you would take it and was only trying to save you pain. I thought it was best that you didn't know, in case…'

'In case? In case what? In case he didn't make it.'

'Yes. I didn't want to raise your hopes or you would be devastated when you had to face reality.'

'I have lived with the reality of what might have happened to him for two years. You say he was ill. How is it that he hasn't been taken before the tribunal of judges and executed before now?'

'As to that I cannot say. The Conciergerie is a huge place and bursting at the seams with prisoners. People get lost and forgotten in there. Maybe that's what happened to your father. What I do know is that he was alive when I left there. I have met with associates employed at the Foreign Office and I am awaiting information from agents in Paris, who make it their business to secure access to information concerning the condemned prisoners from the various prisons throughout Paris. If your father is still in the Conciergerie, then they will know and I will be informed. Until we hear from them there is nothing we can do but wait.'

Delphine was incredulous. 'Wait? But I cannot wait.'

'What else can we do?'

'You need not do anything. If he is still alive, then I will go to France. It is what I do. I have never failed in any of my assignments. Some way, somehow, if he is still in there, I will get him out.'

'You will not,' Laurence stated harshly. 'You are not going nowhere near France. I mean it, Delphine. You will stay here with me and when the reports come through, then we will decide together the best way forward.'

'No. I cannot wait. I will speak with Sir Godfrey. He will know what to do.'

'I have already spoken to Sir Godfrey. He is working to find out what he can.'

'The Foreign Office might help.'

'This is a private matter. There is no funding. Your father is not an English citizen so the powers that be in the Foreign Office will not help us. I know it is difficult, Delphine, but you must be patient. Do not even think of defying me in this.'

'It must have crossed your mind that my father might have died in the Conciergerie and been forgotten.'

'It has, but then again he might not.'

'Not yet—but there is every chance that we might

be too late and he will be taken before the tribunal. He might defend himself as best he can, but he was condemned from the moment they laid hands on him. His crime was that of being a member of the nobility and having lived too well—which is treason to the spirit of the ordinary citizens of France.'

'You know the score. Helping people to escape the Conciergerie could get us imprisoned at the very least. Agents live on borrowed time. We live in the shadows, using anonymity as a shield. The work we do is neither glamorous nor exciting, doing work most people would never consider doing—and all in the name of King and country. What you have achieved in your work I marvel at and I respect and admire your bravery and devotion to duty. But this…' He swallowed and averted his eyes. 'A line must be drawn. I cannot allow you to go to France.'

One look at his face convinced Delphine that he was absolutely furious with her suggestion. Not only were his eyes glittering with icy shards, but the muscles in his cheeks were vibrating to a degree that she had never seen before. She drew an infuriated breath.

'You are a monster, Laurence Beaumont. It is really too much for you to start laying down rules in this lordly fashion. I will not be manipulated and if you insist on being disagreeable, I suggest you tell me what will be done if my father is still alive in the Conciergerie, because I will tell you now that I will not be left behind.' She eyed him suspiciously as she waited for him to speak, recognising that the stern set of his face and the thin line of his lips did not suggest much tolerance. He came to stand in front of her and, when his eyes peered into hers, she could sense the anger behind them.

'I mean what I say. You will not go to France. You will do as I say, Delphine.'

Bravely she tried to face up to him, hoping her voice wouldn't break and trying to hold on to her shattered pride. He had made his feelings plain in the one inimical glance. 'What you mean is that I must learn my place. Yes, I understand you perfectly.' Feeling her control collapsing, she went out, hot tears burning her eyes, the lump in her throat almost choking her.

Still simmering, on reaching her room she paced the carpet as her anger subsided. She would need a clear head in the days ahead if she was going to help her father. Laurence said he would not allow her to go to France. *Well, we shall see about that, my lord.* If he thought he had married a meek-mannered obedient creature who would roll over at his every command like a pet dog, then he was mistaken.

Not only did she resent his high-handed, autocratic commands, but she was still smarting over his treatment of her, for not taking her into his confidence. She wouldn't allow him to go ahead and arrange a foray into France without her. This wasn't how she had imagined their reunion would be, but she had to make a stand now, before he got the idea that he could run roughshod over her. If she allowed him to begin their marriage by commanding her every move, then it didn't bode well for their future.

* * *

Laurence watched her go, tempted to go after her, but he remained motionless. Having made her understand what he expected of her, he told himself she would give up the idea of going to France. The idea that he would allow her to go there alone and without help was unthinkable. And yet she had stood there and defied him. She had stood up to him with a rebellious spirit which, when they had been in France, he would have thought nothing of. And now she was his wife it would seem nothing had changed. She was angry about him keeping what he knew about her father to himself and he could understand that. What he was unprepared for was her threat to defy him and go to France regardless of his refusal to even consider letting her go—and she was foolhardy enough to do just that.

After weeks of missing her, to find her here and seeing her now gave him the most piercing joy of his life. Leaving her had almost torn him apart. With single-minded determination he had immersed himself in both the task of seeing bank managers in the hope that they would be willing to loan him the money for getting his mine working, and speaking to his superiors in the Foreign Office to assist him in getting Delphine's father out of the Conciergerie.

Deeply affected by the harsh words they had exchanged and in no mood to go to bed, he poured himself a brandy, and then another. Finding that he was unable to dull the ache that came with just thinking about Delphine and what she must have gone through in Cornwall after he had left, he went upstairs.

When he had returned home, Carstairs had told him of her arrival and that he'd put her in his mother's bedchamber since it was the only one habitable. Not knowing what to think and wondering what had brought her to London, he'd gone into the drawing room, surprised to find her there.

Now he paused outside her room. Unable to resist the temptation to go inside, he quietly opened the door. Going to the bed, he stood and looked at his sleeping wife curled up in the middle of the bed, unable to believe she was there at all. He stood and silently studied her, thinking he had never seen anything so lovely. His breath caught at the sight of her, the light from the lamp bathing her in its soft light, her features exquisite in its golden glow. She was like a sleeping goddess.

He savoured the delicate lines of her face, the delicious curve of her lips and the thick fan of her dark lashes shadowing her cheeks. Her hair spilled in lovely disarray about her head. The reaction of his body was instantaneous. His loins felt suddenly heavy as he remembered their coupling on the beach. He closed his eyes against the vision.

He felt resentment that following their exchange of angry words she could come to bed and fall asleep like a tired child, while he, feeling hurt and entirely rejected, should have to seek his bed alone.

Presenting herself for breakfast the following morning, she found Laurence was already there. Having little appetite, Delphine helped herself to scrambled eggs and toast from the silver warming dishes on the dresser and went to the table. Standing, Laurence walked round and pulled a chair out for her, making sure she was seated comfortably before going back to his own. One look at his hard expression told her he was still smarting over their argument the previous night.

'You slept well?' Laurence raised one brow in arrogant enquiry as she picked at her eggs.

'Yes, very well. And you?' Stony faced, he nodded. 'I hope you will give serious thought to what we discussed last night, Laurence. I meant what I said. I will not be sidelined from any plans you make about going to France.'

'I have no intention of doing that. I am not doing this to hurt you, Delphine, but you must realise that if we are to help your father, then we can do nothing without a solid plan.'

'I realise that. I am not stupid, Laurence. Is there anything else you wish to say on the matter?'

'Not at present. I'm glad we understand each other.'

'No, Laurence,' she said coldly. 'I understand you, but you do not understand me. Has it not occurred to you that I would have found it easier to adjust to my new position as your wife if, on our wedding day, you had not kept something from me that was of the utmost importance? It shows a callous indifference to my feelings. Let me remind you that as your wife I am equal in all things—not your possession or your chattel, to be told what I will and will not do.'

Laurence gave her a long, speculative look. 'Will you not?'

'No,' she snapped. 'And where my father is concerned, I am prepared to wait until we know more.'

'I'm glad you agree with me on that score,' he said and she was relieved to see some of the tautness leave his face. 'First, we must ascertain that he is still alive. After that I will decide what is to be done.'

'*We* will decide what is to be done,' she amended. 'I meant what I said, Laurence. I will not be kept out of this. If you try to go behind my back, then I will take matters into my own hands and make my own way to Paris.'

'I have already made my feelings plain on that, so, let us agree to discuss this further when we know more,' he said. She nodded stiffly. 'Now,' he continued, casting a disapproving eye over her dress, 'we must do something about your wardrobe.'

She glanced down at her dress. 'Why? What's wrong with it?'

'The dress you are wearing is fine for day wear in Cornwall, but in London as my wife we must do something about it.'

'But we don't have the money to spend on a new wardrobe for me—not when we'll shortly be returning to Cornwall.'

'We are not on the streets yet. I think my bank balance will stretch to some new gowns. My sister will be arriving tomorrow, so she'll advise you.'

Delphine stared at him. 'Your sister? But—you never said…'

'I haven't had the chance.'

'Which sister? I recall you telling me you had two, both in the north of England.'

'Julia lives in Manchester—her husband is in textiles in a big way. He knows I am to sell the house and has shown some interest in buying it. He's been considering a London residence for a while and has always admired this house. It would suit him perfectly.'

'I'm not surprised. It's a fine house.'

'I agree with you, but it all has to go. There are some pieces—paintings and the odd pieces of furniture I'm fond of—that will be packed up and transported to Cornwall. But as for the rest of it—should Julia's husband not buy the house then it will be auctioned off.'

He presided over the rest of the meal with calm composure. He was politely courteous and attentive, making no further mention of their disagreement of the night before and giving no hint of his feelings. But as soon as breakfast was over he excused himself, mentioning some urgent business matter that must be attended to, leaving Delphine to amuse herself and spend another night alone.

Julia arrived the following afternoon. Delphine kept to her room to allow Laurence to receive her alone. It was an emotional moment for brother and sister, the past year of Laurence's incarceration in the Conciergerie uppermost in both their minds. After what she thought to be an appropriate length of time, she went down to meet Julia, entering the drawing room when she was lightly berating her brother for his hasty marriage.

'I'll have you know that I'm dreadfully put out with you for not inviting us to the wedding—and so is Mary, whose two daughters, like my own dear Charlotte, would have loved to be bridesmaids.'

'I'm sorry, Julia. The wedding was in Cornwall—way too far for you to travel at such short notice. However, you are here now so you will have the opportunity of getting to know Delphine.'

'I sincerely hope so.' She turned her attention on Delphine who had just entered. 'Now introduce me to your wife before I grow even more vexed with you.'

Gallantly Laurence took Delphine's hand and drew her forward to perform the honours. 'May I present my lovely wife, Delphine. And this, Delphine, is my incorrigible sister Julia.'

Delphine smiled at the slender woman dressed in a fashionable gown of emerald green and wished she had paid more attention to her own appearance—although the dress she was wearing of a delicate shade of blue was the best that she had. Julia was a pretty brunette, with a delicately arched nose and winged brows over friendly grey eyes. 'It's a pleasure to meet you, Julia—although Laurence didn't tell me you were coming until yesterday.'

'I'm happy to meet you, too,' Julia assured her, her voice warm with obvious sincerity, kissing her lightly on the cheek before drawing her down on to a sofa. 'My brother didn't tell me how pretty you are. Laurence is the youngest in the family—Mary, the eldest, is the one who keeps us all on the straight and narrow. Mary and I have been waiting a long time to see who Laurence would choose for a wife—if at all. We were beginning to give up on him. I would have brought my daughter to meet you. She's eight years old and has developed a passion for horses. Fortunately my husband's parents have a stable full of them so she's gone to stay with them in Derbyshire for the time being.'

'And what has brought you to London at this time, Julia?' Laurence asked as they settled down for refreshment.

'Primarily to see you. We have all been so worried about you in that dreadful French prison. I hope you've put all that behind you now and that your feet are firmly fixed on English soil. I'm sure Delphine will agree with me. But I'm also here to do some shopping. James was too busy to accompany me—but he did tell me to inform you that he has decided to buy the house, Laurence, so that should be a weight off your mind—and it will keep it in the family, so to speak. You will still be able to look on it as a base whenever you are in London. You—do still want to sell, I take it?'

'I do. There's nothing for me in London any more. I'm looking forward to settling in Cornwall—and it's home for Delphine—although she's spent her life going between her father's home in France and her mother's home in Cornwall.'

Julia looked at Delphine with interest. 'You are half-French, Delphine?'

'Yes—from the Auvergne region. I was born there, and my father before me.'

'How interesting—although now we are at war with France and one hears of such terrible atrocities taking place, it must be a difficult time for you. We hear such varied tales that we simply do not know what to believe.'

Over tea and cakes they talked on, Delphine giving away some of her background and Laurence familiarising Julia on what he would be doing in Cornwall. Delphine felt she had met a kindred spirit in Laurence's sister, with the offer of friendship in her eyes. Julia was interested to know all about her as she and Laurence recollected some of their own happy memories from childhood when their parents had taken them to Cornwall.

'Your visit couldn't be more timely,' Laurence said on a change of subject. 'Since you are here to do some shopping, that would settle a problem I have with my wife's wardrobe. When it comes to fashion there's no one more knowledgeable than you, Julia, so I will engage your talents.'

'Why, I'd be delighted.'

'I knew you would. I'm sure you will be able to help her find the perfect gowns—but watch the purse strings. They're shorter than they've ever been.' He gave his sister a knowing look and she nodded. Their father's pursuit of gambling had lasting results.

'Don't worry. You can count on me. I'll soon have Delphine looking like the best dressed lady in London—although,' she said, becoming thoughtful, 'Laurence has told me that you have only recently buried your grandfather, Delphine. Should you not be in mourning?'

'No,' Delphine answered quickly. 'I hate wearing black and dull colours. Besides, my grandfather would not have wanted me to.'

'Well then, that's settled,' Julia said, smiling broadly. 'We'll go shopping tomorrow, and I know just where to take you. I am so looking forward to this.'

After the darkness that had befallen Delphine, with the sorrow of her grandfather's and Aunt Amelia's deaths still fresh in her mind and the fear and apprehension she suffered daily for her father, it was with a heavy heart that she tried to rekindle her spirit and carry on. Until they had news of her father, they were playing a waiting game, and Delphine wasn't very good at waiting.

The atmosphere was strained between her and Laurence. The bond that had strengthened between them in Cornwall now seemed to have been sundered. Laurence was a stranger to her. She could almost feel the invisible barrier he had erected between them. They began to avoid each other. He left her to do whatever she would with her days and spent the evenings at his club, leaving Delphine to sleep alone.

If Julia noticed anything odd in their behaviour, she didn't refer to it. She proved to be Delphine's salvation at this time—a godsend. She was tireless. They went to the shops for fripperies and visited popular modistes to put in motion the making of new gowns post haste. Julia showed her the places of interest and galleries. They drove through Hyde Park. Then there were the evenings. Escorted by Laurence, they attended the theatre, the after-theatre parties and soirées at some grand house.

She became so popular that Laurence remarked that she was becoming a social butterfly. They received an invitation from one of London's elite families to attend a ball in two weeks' time and Julia, extremely excited, began making plans for new ball gowns.

'I can't tell you how happy I am that you married Laurence,' Julia said when they were returning home in the carriage from a trip to the shops. 'He used to be a popular man about town—which seems so long ago now. I know he was taken prisoner in France and I can only imagine what he went through—but he is back now and I hope he will settle down and not be persuaded to return to France. I'm glad he's going to live in Cornwall and leave the London scene behind.'

'So am I,' Delphine agreed. 'This is my first time in London and I have to say I would not like to live here permanently. I would miss Cornwall too much.'

'I find it amazing that we never met when we were at Pendene,' Julia said, 'although I imagine you would be in France when we were there. Laurence never stops telling me how much he admires you. Can you really fire a gun?'

'Yes,' Delphine admitted. 'My father taught me—I think it was because he wanted to take me on the hunts and have some competition when he fired at targets.'

'And is that what happened? Did you?'

'What—give him competition?' She shook her head. 'Not really, although I had a good aim and always managed to hit the target. My uncle taught me how to fence—which I enjoyed and was rather good at.'

'I, too, enjoyed to fence, although I never took it seriously. When he had no one else to practise with Laurence would let me be his partner—but he always took it seriously. Later, as an agent of the Crown, he was trained in combat with edged weaponry, learning defensive tactics and skills so he became good at it. He was quite ruthless and told me I wasn't good enough, so I had to be content to practise my fencing with Mary.'

'Then perhaps we could find time for some jousting—if we can find some swords, that is.'

'There are some at the house. It would be fun—although it's been a long time since I handled a sword. I'll look forward to it, Delphine.'

As one day ran into another, Laurence became even more withdrawn. There was a worried, preoccupied look in his eyes and Delphine could tell by his manner and the way he continued to avoid her that he had something on his mind. She felt sure something was afoot and resentment burned through her all the sharper when she recalled how, despite her insistence that she be kept informed of all developments concerning her father, he was being less than open with her. She felt a betrayal of her trust. What had he learned that he had to be secretive about? Perhaps in his arrogance he considered it was his male prerogative to conceal information that was not considered female business.

The night of the ball arrived. Having sat for what seemed like hours before her dressing table mirror, watching as her maid had painstakingly arranged her heavy hair into an elegant coiffure, deftly twisting it into elaborate curls and teasing soft tendrils over her ears, Delphine was relieved when she had finished.

Julia came to help her into her gown of rose silk, designed in sophisticated, simple lines. Cut low, the gentle swell of her breasts rising above the bodice, the shimmering silk fell in artful folds to her feet and set off her figure to perfection. She turned this way and that to survey her reflection.

'What do you think, Julia? Will I do?'

'Yes,' Julia said. 'You look just perfect and you will catch all the eyes tonight. Any man, even those in their dotage, who sees you tonight, looking as you do, will surely find their heart going into its final palpitation—as will Prince George himself. Those who haven't seen you yet will be asking who you are, and there will be many handsome young men begging for the honour to be introduced, so for your own safety I advise you not to drift far from Laurence's side.

'Now, where is that handsome brother of mine?'

she wondered, going to the door just as Laurence was coming in. 'Ah, there you are. Come and admire your beautiful wife while I go and put the finishing touches to my own appearance.'

Delphine met his eyes in the mirror as he came to stand behind her. Attired in a dark blue suit and his dark hair neatly combed, there was a special radiance about him. She could not take her eyes off him while her heart began to soar. Being with him, close to him once more, was pure heaven.

'I have something for you—something that will put the finishing touches to that lovely dress you are wearing.' He presented her with a beautiful pearl necklace and matching drop earrings. As he fastened the pearls around her neck, he could not have guessed at the depth of feeling bottled up inside her.

Delphine continued to watch him through the mirror and, feeling his fingers on her flesh, despite her hurt and general desire to know what it was that was keeping them apart, she was filled with a disturbing surge of lust for him.

'You look lovely, Delphine. You will be the belle of the ball tonight.'

'You flatter me, Laurence.' Moving away from him, she picked up her gloves and velvet cloak. Handing it to him, she stood still while he folded it about her shoulders. Leaving the room, they proceeded down the stairs. 'Every woman who is to attend the ball tonight will have done their utmost to look their best. Julia tells me Prince George is expected to be there.'

'Yes, so I've heard. If so, then I will make a point of introducing you. Would that be agreeable to you?'

'Of course. Who wouldn't wish to be introduced to a royal prince?'

Chapter Eleven

Laurence escorted the two ladies to Piccadilly in his midnight-blue town coach drawn by four bay horses, which tossed their heads as they joined the stream of traffic going in the same direction as themselves. Although the autumn season had only just begun, the elite of society had contrived to be in time to be present at the Pickfords' ball.

On entering the Palladian-style mansion, they were met by a wave of light and heat, perfume and strains of music coming from the ballroom. Laurence steered them through the crush of the hall into a large salon, which was full to overflowing. It was adorned with huge banks of ferns and exotic flowers sent that very morning from the hot houses of the Pickfords' country residence in Surrey and glittered at its most brilliant in the light of immense crystal chandeliers ablaze with innumerable candles. It was filled with the noise of conversation, punctuated by the flutter of fans and the swish of trains brushing the carpets.

After drinking a glass of champagne offered to them by a white-gloved footman, they proceeded up the grand staircase to the ballroom, where their distinguished hosts stood ready to receive their guests. The orchestra was playing a country dance and already couples were making free with the lively steps.

Despite the cloud Laurence was living under, he could not have been happier escorting Delphine to her first ball. Before the revolution in France, she told him she had enjoyed attending functions with her French relatives. When they had taken her to Paris, as young as she had been, she had enjoyed attending the many social functions continually held in the nation's capital and had looked forward to enjoying the same in London.

Tonight gave her even more reason to enjoy herself, to have the eyes of everyone upon her. The finery and flattery delighted her and she would snap her fingers at anyone who showed their dislike of her. Laurence could see she loved to dance and she did so with a natural grace which delighted him. He had also discovered that she could sing and play the piano in a strange untutored way which was somehow more effective than if she had been taught by a maestro.

Her moods were like quicksilver and unpredictable, but whether she was aloof and frosty or wickedly appealing, she drew men to her side almost without conscious effort, men Laurence soon sent packing if they showed any sign of being over-familiar.

As he awaited news from Sir Godfrey concerning

her father, the tension between them had become unbearable. If he was still alive in the Conciergerie, then Laurence would leave immediately for France. Delphine was adamant that she would go with him, but he could not take the risk of losing her should they be caught and arrested. She asked constantly if he had any information and every time he sidestepped the question.

Relieved that he had lowered his guard at last and hoping it would continue, a sigh of relief slipped from Delphine's lips as Laurence swept her smoothly around the ballroom, continually turning in ever-widening circles until the faces of those who watched became an indistinct blur beyond his broad shoulders.

'You are enjoying the ball, Delphine?'

She laughed, evidencing now only her relief that he seemed more relaxed towards her, and her pleasure at being able to dance for the first time with her husband. 'Very much.'

He looked at her upturned face, a teasing smile twitching at his lips. 'You dance divinely, by the way. You are as light as thistledown in my arms.'

'I feel as if I'm floating on a cloud,' she said as he whirled her round in the light of the crystal chandeliers, which left her head spinning and her senses reeling. The warmth of a blush seared her cheeks as he held her tighter.

'That might be the champagne you have drunk.' A wicked, devilish grin stretched across his lips—it was a look she had despaired of seeing again. At that moment, nothing existed beyond her husband's encircling arms and the endless glitter of green eyes that held hers captive. Having missed him from her bed, there was a warm, underlying excitement that Laurence had kindled in her from the beginning—a promise and a tingle of anticipation of that moment when she would be alone with him once more.

When the dance was over, Laurence did not relinquish her hand.

'Come, the Prince of Wales has arrived. I will introduce you.'

Side by side they walked out of the ballroom to where a group of gentlemen clustered round the heir to the throne, talking merrily and imbibing their chosen tipple. On seeing Laurence they parted and greeted him as one of the Prince's intimate circle. Some of them were preening fops and dressed as colourfully as peacocks, and when they opened their mouths it was to laugh inanely at some amusing comment.

The future king, a fun-loving, courteous man of the world, was dressed in a magnificent suit of emerald-green velvet richly embroidered in gold. He had a considerable presence and a certain majesty, but with a voracious appetite for wine, women and food, in his early thirties, his body was beginning to fill out. Everyone in England knew he had married a woman, Maria Fitzherbert, a marriage that was invalid under English civil law because his father, King George III, had not consented to it.

On seeing Laurence, he smiled broadly. 'Ah, Lord

Beaumont! Welcome back from wherever it is you've been. I heard you were in France—you were gone so long we were beginning to think you had perished over there.'

'Now what would I be doing across the water, Your Highness, when we are at war?'

'Exactly—although why any Englishman would go to a country where the people murder their King and Queen and all the nobility is a mystery to me. What a terrible state of affairs.'

'I couldn't agree more. As a matter of fact I've been down in Cornwall,' Laurence informed him—he never spoke about his work other than to people of the same occupation. 'I've inherited some property down there, a pleasant prospect, and I've decided to move there.' Turning to Delphine and taking her hand, he drew her forward. 'I would like to introduce my wife. Lady Beaumont is from Cornwall.'

Delphine made her curtsy and, smiling benevolently at the young woman, the Prince condescendingly took her hand and helped raise her to her feet. She found herself meeting a commanding gaze and sensual lips.

'I am more than happy to meet you, Lady Beaumont.' He glanced towards Laurence, a vinous flush spreading over his features. 'Your bride is ravishing, Beaumont. By God, if I were not already well provided for in a wife, I do believe I might steal her away from you myself. Charming she is, simply charming. All my good wishes to you both for a long and fruitful life.'

'I thank Your Highness. You are very gracious,' Delphine said softly, stepping back.

More loud talk and laughter ensued, the Prince's pleasant but rather foolish laughter rising above it all.

Laurence made his excuse to leave and escorted Delphine to the supper room, collecting Julia, who was gossiping with an acquaintance, on the way.

Back on the dance floor with another over-enthusiastic partner, Delphine watched Laurence closely. The image of relaxed elegance, he stood with his shoulder resting against one of the pillars around the dance floor, his eyes following her every move-ment. There was a moment when his expression was unguarded, his face a brooding mask. And suddenly he wasn't there.

Delphine did a quick sweep of the ballroom—he appeared to have disappeared. Not until the dance was over and her partner had gone did she go in search of him. He wasn't in the card room, or the supper room. Deciding to seek out Julia and passing the top of the stairs, she glanced down into the hall, seeing her husband in the company of two gentlemen.

They stood close together and seemed to be in se-rious conversation. She stood and watched them for a moment, seeing one of the gentlemen pass Lau-rence some papers, which he slipped inside his coat. Puzzled, she turned away when she was claimed by Julia, who took her aside to introduce her to some of her friends. Her intuition told her that something was afoot and, curiosity getting the better of her, she went in search of Laurence. She found him in one of the rooms set aside for cards and dice and any other game that caught one's interest, but he was showing no interest in what was being played.

'Here you are, Laurence. It's difficult to pin you down among all these people.' If he'd looked closer, he would see there was a storm brewing inside her. Her cheeks had gone pale and her lips were drawn in a thin line. 'Take me outside, will you? I would like some air and a little time alone with my husband.'

'Anything to oblige.' Taking her arm, he escorted her out of the tall French doors on to the terrace.

A mix of summer flowers filled the gardens beyond and in the glowing light of the moon, dark places shadowed clandestine trysts. Insects could be heard above whispered declarations of those hidden from sight. Laurence drew Delphine further along the terrace to a place which offered complete privacy and the subtle scent of roses and honeysuckle was heavy on the air.

'You are angry, Delphine.'

'How observant of you. Who were those gentlemen you were talking to in the hall? I saw you with them when I came out of the ballroom.'

His face hardened. 'Acquaintances. Why?'

'You were deep in serious conversation. I was curious.' She stood by the ornate stone balustrade and watched him pace slowly up and down. He was uneasy about something, that was plain.

'Laurence,' she said irritably, 'can you please stand still for a minute and talk to me? What is this?

Please tell me.' Instinct sent her towards him, but she stopped herself. 'I am not stupid. There is something afoot and I would appreciate you being honest with me. Tell me what it is. I saw them pass some papers to you. What were they?'

Laurence took a step away from her and averted his eyes. His face looked taut and a muscle tightened beneath his jaw. And then she knew. She felt the colour drain from her face.

'I think I know. They were the papers you will need for you to go to France. You've heard something concerning my father, haven't you? I think you had better tell me. Is he still alive?'

Turning his head and looking at her intently, he nodded. 'Yes. He is.'

'I knew it.' Delphine stared at him, welcoming this news with all her heart. But why had Laurence kept this from her—yet again? 'When were you going to tell me? Or were you going to keep it from me?'

'I haven't kept it from you. I have only just heard myself.'

'When were you going to tell me?'

'I was waiting for a more opportune moment, until—'

Her head snapped up, her eyes glittering with outrage at this insult to her intelligence. 'Until what? Until you managed to sneak away without me?'

'Until we were back at the house,' he told her sharply.

'I thought I'd made it plain when I arrived that I must be included at all times with matters concerning my father. It's disrespectful and cruel to keep this from me.'

Laurence glanced around with a frown. 'Lower your voice, Delphine. You forget yourself.'

His words increased her anger and her eyes sparked like chipped ice. '*I* forget myself? You are the one to have deceived me and yet you have the gall to tell me not to forget *my*self!'

'Stop it,' he said sharply. 'You go too far.'

Frustration exploded within Delphine. 'Do I, indeed? I have shocked you, have I not? I have suddenly turned out to be a woman who is not afraid to speak out. Clearly you thought me too naive and stupid to challenge you, that I cannot think and feel—that you want to do it for me.'

'Now you are being ridiculous.'

As straight as a slender slither of steel, she moved away from him without releasing his eyes. 'You are planning to go to France without me, aren't you, Laurence? How dare you conspire to do this without my knowledge? How dare you?'

'Delphine, I understand that you are upset…'

'Once again, I am not upset, I am furious.' She set her hands on her hips, glaring at him. 'How could you do that?'

He sighed, perching his hip on the stone balustrade. 'Because I am thinking of you. I cannot permit you to go with me.'

'You cannot forbid me to go.'

'I can and I will. I want to protect you. Can't you understand that?'

'Yes, I can and I admire you for it. But you must face the fact that one way or another I will go.' Her eyes flared with anger. 'If you are arrested and thrown back into the Conciergerie or some other godforsaken prison in Paris, I suppose I'll have to go and try to get you out.'

'I don't intend being arrested, but should I be that unfortunate, you will not set foot on French soil. Is that understood, Delphine?'

She glared at him. 'No, it is not. I will not be dictated to, Laurence. While you are locked away I will be on my own. You will be in no position to give me orders. You won't *be* here to stop me. It isn't certain that you will make it back.'

He saw the defiance in her eyes and a hard, disquieting line settled between Laurence's eyes. 'No, it isn't, but it's a chance I have to take. Hopefully all will go well and I will soon be home—with your father. I am sorry it has to be this way and you have a perfect right to be angry, but whatever happens you will remain here. Should anything happen to me you will be notified.'

'And who will do that?'

'The Foreign Office.'

'And with that I have to be content. I have seen the dangers with my own eyes and I have no desire to become a widow before I've had the chance to be a wife.'

Laurence's eyebrows rose in amazement, then dropped swiftly and ferociously into a frown. 'Stop this foolishness, Delphine. There's no need for all this melodrama.'

She moved forward to confront him with her own anger. 'Melodrama? I am many things, but never dramatic. What you like or dislike is of supreme indifference to me just now.' She smoothed her skirt as if to straighten her thoughts. The atmosphere between them was beginning to weigh on her. She was tired and her head was aching. 'If you don't mind, I would like to leave now. It's been a long evening and I have a headache. It's over for me.'

He nodded. 'Very well. If you're sure. I'll arrange to have the carriage brought to the front of the house.'

'Thank you. I'll go and find Julia.'

The day following the Pickfords' ball, having received a message from Sir Godfrey that he had important matters to discuss, Laurence entered White's. Joining him at his table and ordering a brandy, he listened carefully as Sir Godfrey told him that the plans for him going to Paris had changed. The assignment was not something Laurence could carry out by himself. He had been notified by a reliable source that Henri St Clair was frail in both mind and body. Laurence could not get him out of France alone. Perhaps it was time to involve Delphine after all.

Laurence shook his head. 'I cannot involve Delphine in this. I have told her that her father is still in the Conciergerie, but I have forbidden her to accompany me.'

'I can well imagine how she reacted to that.'

'And you would be right.'

'Your need to protect your wife is understandable. But you must face the fact that one way or another you will need someone alongside you. You cannot do this alone. Henri St Clair is in a bad way and will need taking care of. You will have to relent and allow Delphine to go with you. More than anyone she knows that choices in such times have consequences. She knows that if she is taken prisoner she can expect no mercy.'

'Which is precisely why I don't want to involve her.'

'It's dangerous, Lord Beaumont. But think of it. In the past Delphine has managed to get many people out of France—one way or another. She will not thank you for going it alone. And should you fail, she will never forgive you.'

Laurence nodded, a hard look on his face as he thought carefully about what Sir Godfrey was saying. 'You are right, of course,' he said, relenting at last. 'I will make arrangements to leave at once. The risk of Henri St Clair being taken for trial increases daily.'

'I agree.' Feeling inside his coat, Sir Godfrey produced a sealed package and handed it to him. 'I was hoping you would change your mind. Those are papers for you both. You know what to do.'

It was a deeply troubled Laurence who arrived back at the house. Making his way to the salon, he was surprised to find his wife and sister indulging in a fencing match. The carpet had been rolled back. He entered quietly, unnoticed by the pair of duellists, their identities hidden by facial masks. His attention was gripped by the woman who was his wife, her figure lithesome as she fought with the skill and address of an experienced duellist, moving with an extraordinary grace, as if movement were a pleasure to her. His sister was good, but not as skilled as Delphine.

Propping his shoulder against the doorpost, he watched with interest as they parried and thrust, moving ceaselessly about the highly polished parquet floor. He folded his arms, with a slight smile on his lips, and his unswerving gaze now watched his wife's every move, feasting on the graceful lines of her slim hips. To allow more movement she had done away with the encumbrance of petticoats and the fabric of her skirt clung to her incredibly long legs. She was, Laurence realised, a skilled swordswoman, with faultless timing and stunningly executed moves. There was an aura of confidence and daring about her that drew all his attention.

Still unaware of his presence, when Julia lost her grip on her sword and it clattered to the floor, Delphine suddenly cried enough and whipped off her mask to reveal her laughing, shining face.

'I think that's enough for one day, Julia. You fence very well—although we are both somewhat rusty. We'll fence some more tomorrow, if you like.'

She was breathless and her cheeks were flushed, her eyes a brilliant dancing amber. Her abundance of hair was tied loosely on top of her head, with riotous locks tumbling about all over the place. To Laurence at that moment she looked like a bandit princess, vibrant with health and life. His eyes soaked up the sight of her, for which he was more thirsty than water by far.

Julia was the first to become aware of Laurence's presence. She removed her face guard and breastplate, her face breaking into a welcoming smile. 'Laurence! I didn't realise we had company. How long have you been standing there?'

'Long enough. I was enjoying watching you. I didn't want to interrupt such fine swordplay.'

'As you will have seen,' she said, turning towards Delphine, 'your wife is more than a match for me. I'm no longer as agile as I was. She has much to teach me.'

Delphine crossed to them. 'I didn't know you were there, Laurence.'

He smiled. 'I'm glad. You are an excellent swordswoman. Had you been aware of my presence, I may have distracted you.'

Her sudden smile had a warmth to contend with the glowing sun slanting through the windows. 'You are mistaken. I fence the same regardless of whether I have an audience or not. I thought you had business in town. I did not expect you back quite so soon.'

'I have a matter of some importance to discuss with you.'

'Then I will leave you both to it,' Julia said. 'I feel the need to go to my room to freshen up.'

'Thank you for the practice, Julia. I enjoyed it.'

Delphine looked at Laurence. 'I think I'll go and change. When I come back down we can talk.'

'Not so fast,' he said as she was about to turn away. 'I have a desire to test your fencing skills for myself.' He cocked her a smile. 'That's if you're up to it?'

'I'm tougher than I look.'

'So am I.'

He quickly divested himself of his coat and waistcoat, rolling back his shirtsleeves over powerful forearms. Removing his cravat and shirt stud to allow more freedom, he began fastening himself into the breastplate discarded by Julia. He was looking at her with just a gleam of mischief at the back of his impassive handsome face. 'So you court danger, do you, Delphine?'

'All the time, Laurence—as well you know. Do you fence often?'

'Why do you ask?'

'I'm curious as to how skilled an adversary you will make.'

Laurence crossed the room to help himself to one of the fine weapons on display in a glass-fronted cabinet. 'Not as often as I would like.'

'In which case I imagine you'll be a bit rusty,' she taunted, with an innocent smile curving her lips.

His grin was roguish and the gleam in his eyes more so as his hand closed over the hilt of a weapon with a strong, slender blade. 'Imagine anything you like, my dear wife,' he retorted, flexing the supple blade between his hands before swishing the air in a practised arc, 'but my infrequence at practice does not mean that I shall be complacent or clumsy, or in need of lessons in self-defence.'

'That may be so, but I don't think this will take long.'

'So—you are planning to thrash me, are you?' he drawled, one brow arrogantly raised.

'Soundly.'

Donning a face mask, Laurence advanced towards her. Delphine did the same. 'I do hope your vision is not impaired by the mask,' he taunted.

'Rest assured, I can see perfectly well.'

'I'm glad to hear it,' he remarked with a supremely arrogant smile, one to which his wife would take exception to under different circumstances. 'But don't complain afterwards that I didn't warn you.' He spoke with tolerant amusement. 'Prepare to defend yourself, Lady Beaumont, or I swear I will pin you to the wall.'

'I will not give you the chance, Lord Beaumont. The challenge to participate in a sport that is as pleasurable to me as riding a horse is much too tempting to resist.'

With a vivacious laugh she replaced her mask and picked up her rapier. In one swift movement she was in the centre of the room and Laurence found himself engaged. Before the mask hid her features, he saw there was a feverish flush on her cheeks and a wild determined light shone in her eyes. She moved skilfully, confident she could best him, but careful not to underestimate his ability.

Laurence was an excellent sportsman and accounted an excellent blade, but he soon realised he had his work cut out as his slender, darting opponent left no opening in her unwavering guard. The bright blade seemed to be everywhere at once, multiplied a hundred times by her supple wrists. But Laurence didn't make it easy for her. He fought with skill, continually circling his opponent, changing his guard a dozen times, but Delphine never failed to parry adroitly in her own defence.

Laurence could imagine the face behind the mask—the excitement of the fight would have put more colour into her cheeks, a gleam in her eyes and a rosiness on her full lips. The image sent desire surging through him as foils rang together, meeting faster and faster as he forced her to a killing pace. Sweat now soaked her fine silk bodice so that it clung alluringly to her arms and he could well imagine how the tender swell of her breasts would be outlined behind the breastplate.

Delphine was beginning to weaken, finding herself held at bay by a superior strength. Laurence knew this and with a low chuckle doubled his agility. He parried her beautifully executed riposte with force sufficient to knock the weapon from her grip. He pointed the button-tipped foil at her throat.

'Do you accept surrender?'

Accepting she was beaten, Delphine whipped her mask away, breathing hard. 'I do. I was beaten fair and square. You have made good your threat. No doubt you regret wasting your time on such a weak opponent.'

'Nonsense. You were already weakened by your

bout with Julia.' Removing his mask and breastplate, he thought how truly adorable she looked in complete disarray.

'You are too generous. There are no excuses for my defeat. I was beaten by a superior strength. I accept that.'

'A master?' he pressed, with a broad, arrogant smile.

'You conceited beast. I refuse to flatter your vanity further.'

Laurence's grin was wicked. 'And you are magnanimous in defeat? I look forward to a repeat of the exercise.'

'Next time you will not be so lucky,' she quipped, with a jaunty impudence Laurence found utterly exhilarating.

'I'm looking forward to it already. Who taught you to fence?'

'My uncle,' she said, placing the rapiers back in the cabinet. 'You said you had something of import to discuss with me. I'll go to my room and change. I must look a fright.'

Lifting his gaze from his wife's feminine curves, slowly Laurence let his eyes seek hers. His amusement had vanished. An aura of anticipation surrounded them. It was blatantly sensual and keenly felt by them both.

Laurence's firm mouth curved in a sensuous smile. 'Believe me, there is nothing wrong with the way you look, Delphine.'

Delphine flushed and smiled tremulously. 'Not to you, maybe, but I do need to change.'

'I'll come with you.' She gave him a sharp look. He shook his head. 'I wish to speak with you in private. There is a chance of us being overheard in here or Julia might return.'

Laurence sat in a chair and watched Delphine swill her burning face with cold water. Her hands went to the back of her dress, awkwardly fumbling with the tiny buttons. Seeing her lack of progress, he stood up and spun her around, sweeping her hair out of the way as his hands proceeded to unfasten the tiny loops from the buttons with ease. Slipping the dress from her shoulders and down past her waist, he helped her step out of it, discarding it over a chair.

Aware that what he had to tell her was of the utmost seriousness and that he must marshal his emotions with ruthless command, trying to steady his racing heart and not to dwell on how delectable she looked standing there with the minimum of clothes and her hair draped over one shoulder, he returned to the chair and sat down. Despite the unsettling elements of his mission, he could not, would not ponder a future without Delphine. Yet if anything went wrong then he could lose her for ever.

In his mind he recalled the moment they met outside the Conciergerie, when he had realised the person who had come to save him was a woman. In that instant everything changed. She had roused in him feelings he had thought dead to him in that terrible place of incarceration—his sense of honour and duty, his need to defend, to protect. But that was not all. His beautiful saviour had touched him in ways he could never have imagined, summoning passions of desire unlike any he'd ever known.

And yet if she accompanied him on this assignment, the mystical magic that Delphine had weaved about him in her own special way could end in a fragment of time. But Sir Godfrey was right. He could not keep this from her. It was her right to know and she would never forgive him if he failed.

'Well?' she said, dabbing her face dry and turning to look at him. Myriad emotions danced in her eyes. 'What is it you have to say to me? You look serious, Laurence, which tells me it is of the utmost importance.'

'It is. What I am about to ask of you is of a serious nature and I ask you to consider it very carefully.'

'You're scaring me. Tell me.'

'I've altered my opinion and you can come with me to France.'

Delphine stiffened. 'France? But—I thought you said...?'

'I've changed my mind. I have spoken to Sir Godfrey and he has told me I will need help to get your father out.'

She stared at him. 'He—he—is he very ill?'

'He is in a weakened state. That is all I know. Believe me, Delphine, I don't want you to do this, but you are the obvious person. You speak fluent French for a start.' He stood up and moved to stand directly in front of her, encouraged that she did not step away from him. 'You have confidence, too, as well as a sense of humour—although I have seen very little of that of late—which is probably my fault. And your compassion for others compels my admiration and respect.'

Delphine trembled, staring at him.

'You are also brave,' he continued as she folded her arms across her chest and turned away abruptly. 'The fact that you have worked your way through adversity in France and the care you take to save the lives of others is commendable and bespeaks your courage and good sense. You're like a force of nature— a young woman who thinks nothing of breaking the rules of convention. But this is not about kissing a young man in the middle of a dance floor or defying the rules of society. This is a war and you can expect no mercy if you are caught. I know I can trust you, trust in your integrity, which is a rarity for me. It is not often I come across a person I can trust.'

Rendered helpless by his words, Delphine turned and look at him. 'It's difficult to argue with a man who praises me not for superficial things, but for the very qualities that I most value in myself. It would seem you do understand me a little better than I have given you credit for. It is considerate of you to make me appear so appealing, but entirely unnecessary, I assure you.'

He offered her a smile. 'You still want to go to France with me?' he asked, trying not to think how delectable she looked in her flimsy undergarments revealing her perfect shape beneath.

'Do you need to ask?'

'No. You know how dangerous this will be—you, more than anyone, should know that. What we do is never as simple as black and white.' Dangerous was an understatement.

She was silent for a long moment. 'Yes, I do. I knew that the moment I set foot in France for the first time since my father sent me to live with Grandfather that my life would change. I had to live undercover. I was not able to spend more than one night in one place. I could trust no one. I was not Delphine St Clair at all any more—I was Sophie. There would always be someone searching for people like me and if they found me...' Even as she said the words, Laurence knew that, as brave as she had been—risking her life—when she had been there, likely to be caught at any moment, there were times when she would have been scared and afraid... Something he could understand because he had felt the same way.

'I hope you never know how fragile you are, Delphine.'

'I'm not fragile.'

He gave a wry smile. 'We are all fragile. It's one thing we learn in war. It won't be easy.'

'It never was.'

'After much planning and preparation, I am ready to go ahead. Sir Godfrey is providing his assistance and knowledge of what is going on over there. He's made contact with agents in Paris who will assist if need be. If it is at all possible they will try to get him out and place him in a safe house until we reach Paris. If not, then the same procedure to have me released will be followed, but whereas we headed west to Granville, this time we will be using Calais.'

'I know it will be dangerous. But think of it. I have managed to get many people out of France—one way or another. You must accept that I am perfectly capable of looking after myself. I don't frighten easily. In the past, whenever I have taken an assignment, I had to lie to those I loved and always be afraid. I had to live that way. What I did was my choice.' She lifted her chin and looked him in the eyes. 'I will do anything to save my father. When do we leave?'

'In the morning, at first light.'

'The sooner the better. Thank you for doing this and for caring.' Suddenly she smiled and moved closer to him, a warm, intimate glow in her eyes. 'Now, until it is time for us to go down to dinner,' she said, her eyes delving into his and touching his cheek with the tip of her finger, 'you have been neglectful of me for too long. Is it not time for us to consummate our marriage? I would appreciate some moments of your time.'

Laurence smiled. Delphine stayed close and he felt for her mouth and kissed her tentatively several times until she parted her lips. They kissed slowly as Delphine slipped the straps of her chemise from her shoulder and let it fall to the floor.

'Delphine,' Laurence whispered, stroking her shoulders and back. He pressed himself against her, beathing in her silky perfume, kissed her collarbone and slender neck, her chin and moist mouth. Her nipples were hard and her stomach fluttering with her rapid breathing. Looking seriously into his eyes, she pulled him with her towards the bed.

'You are right to chastise me. I have neglected you of late and we have much to catch up on.' His voice was low, incredibly warm and seductive as he knelt over her naked form.

She smiled, an alluring little smile that dimpled her cheeks. 'Then what are you waiting for?'

They had first made love on the beach at Tregannon, but this was the first time they had made love since their marriage. It was like exploring uncharted territory and Laurence took the time to notice how satiny soft her flesh was, how her skin seemed to quiver under his touch. He loved to touch her. He never wanted to leave her body. He brushed his fingers across her taut breasts and felt the nipples spring to prominence under his hands. He kissed her soft mouth, feeling her lips tremble and then finally parted helplessly, allowing him full rein.

And then their bodies began to take over from their minds and they both wanted more.

Lying in the tangle of sheets when Laurence had left her, Delphine sighed with an enormous contentment, her body rosy and drugged with passions spent. Her eyes had the look of a woman who was utterly fulfilled—of the heart, the mind and the flesh.

After days of tension and avoidance of each other, their argument had ended in a burst of passion and the tenuous bonds of a new relationship, based on friendship as well as carnal desire, had been established. Trust would have to be worked on during the days and weeks ahead, as they learned more about each other, exploring and strengthening, but it would come. That she was sure of.

Chapter Twelve

At first light the following morning, Laurence and Delphine were dressed in dark, sombre attire and equipped with a change of clothes and other necessary things they would need for the journey. Travelling in his coach drawn by four bay horses, they began their journey to Dover where they would acquire a vessel to take them to France.

Ensconced in the well-padded interior and surrounded by claret-coloured cushions, Delphine stared out indifferently as they left London behind to a more pastoral landscape. The day was fine and it was a relief to be setting off at last. She was focused on the purpose that was taking her to France and her uneasiness and concern for what lay ahead was sharper than ever. As the coach rattled and jolted its tedious way over the bad roads, the journey seemed endless.

When at last they reached Dover, darkness had fallen across the land and the stretch of water that separated England from France.

They were to stay the night at an inn Laurence had used often in the past. It also offered good stabling for his horses and the driver would be accommodated at the inn to await their return. Other travellers and locals sat around drinking and eating. Laurence went to talk with the innkeeper as Delphine went to sit at a table in the corner.

'There is a vessel leaving for Calais early in the morning,' Laurence informed her as he took a seat across from her. 'We should arrive some time during the afternoon.'

'What then? Do we take the post to Paris?'

'There will be a carriage waiting for us. It is arranged. This might be a private assignment, Delphine, but I have friends working secretly in France and they are happy to assist me in any way they can to bring your father out of that infernal prison. Always, among my fellow associates in Paris, transport and other arrangements usually run like clockwork. The journey to Paris may be taxing, with every town gate manned by citizens stopping all comers.'

'But we have papers.'

'Sir Godfrey saw to that. We will be doomed if they are suspected to be false.'

'They look authentic to me. We are English, man and wife. You are a wine merchant, travelling to the Ardennes on business. Even in these troubled times there is constant business communication between the French and English merchants.'

'That's because in view of the heavy duties imposed on wines and spirits by the English King and his government, the French are enormously pleased to think of them being cheated out of their revenues by English smugglers.'

Delphine raised her eyebrows. 'And you intend to portray yourself as a smuggler should you be questioned?'

A smile tugged at his lips. 'I might—should I decide to put Tregannon cove to good use.'

'Are you expecting trouble?'

'It's hard to say until we get there. It may not be as difficult getting to Paris as it will be travelling back to Calais. They will be suspicious of everyone travelling in the direction of the coast.'

'In which case we must convince them that we are sympathetic to the revolution and support the good citizens of France.'

They were served food and drink, which Delphine accepted gratefully as her stomach growled for nourishment. After they had eaten they went to their room. It had been a long day and they were both tired, with nerves stretched tight and anxiety heavy on their minds—but not so tired that they couldn't make love. They sank into the bed and into each other's arms. Laurence's mouth was warm and it tasted of wine, and had lost none of its skill in rousing Delphine to a turmoil of desire.

The next day dawned fair. They made their way down to the pier and as Delphine set foot on the boat on this clear morning, her heart was full of hope. Revived by the fresh sea air and deaf to the splash of the boat as it ploughed its way through the water, she turned her back on Dover's white cliffs and fixed her eyes on the distant shore of Calais—a hazy, thin strip of land on the horizon.

During all her missions to France to rescue those wishing to flee the terror, she had suffered, endured and shed tears in her search for her father. Now she was on her way to Paris to save him. No more interminable roads to travel. From the moment Laurence had told her that her father had been found, he had given her his full attention and she was glad to have him by her side.

It was hard for Delphine to imagine, as she set foot on French soil once more, the hideous revolution taking place in the beautiful capital. Fear lurked in the eyes of the people and they were careful lest a word uttered in innocence might be taken out of context and used against them in the future.

A carriage was waiting for them at a designated place and, with Laurence taking the reins, they left the coast and began their three-hundred-mile journey to Paris. They passed through villages where gates were manned by watchful citizen patriots in red caps and sporting the tricoloured cockades. Here, all travellers were stopped. Presenting their papers, being eyed with sly distrust, they were allowed to go on their way.

At last they reached Paris, passing through the gate without attracting too much attention. The streets were thronged with pedestrians and traffic alike and pamphleteers shouting the latest news hot off the press. People hung about in groups, talking loudly about politics and the latest price of bread and anything else that could be discussed and argued over. Some fell silent and cast suspicious eyes their way until they had passed by. A shudder ran through Delphine's body. Instantly she felt Laurence's hand tighten on her arm, reassuring.

He bent close to her ear. 'Don't be afraid, my love. Nothing will happen to you—not while you are with me.'

Delphine knew well enough that he was making an uncertain prediction, but there was no uncertainty about his tone. His words were firm and bold, and she believed, irrationally, that nothing would happen to her while he was there to see that nothing did happen. She glanced about with little enthusiasm. 'I little thought I would be back in Paris so soon.'

'We'll make for the house where I've arranged to meet a friend of mine.'

'Is he a British agent?'

'Yes. William Faulkner. You'll like him. We've known each other for years—we were at Oxford together. He's the youngest of five brothers, so very little comes his way from the family coffers. He did consider soldiering, but that profession didn't attract him.'

'So he became a spy instead.'

'Exactly.'

'And he is a good friend?'

'The best. I would trust him with my life.' He

spoke the truth. They had gone through the long years of training together, enduring punishing regimes and iron discipline, lessons turning them into gentlemen and spies as well as cold-blooded assassins so they would be toughened up for what lay ahead. 'He was in London when I arrived. I was lucky to catch up with him for he was on his way back to Paris. When he was told of our marriage and your search for your father, he offered to help in any way he could. I told him he had been in the Conciergerie for some time and he said he would make enquiries.'

'Then he may have fresh information.'

The Rue Saint-Antoine was noisy and bustling with people. The house was located down in the intricate network of streets and alleyways, close to the river and not far from the Conciergerie. It was a small house, nothing out of the ordinary, just one that was ideally placed as a meeting house for those working for British Intelligence.

Laurence knocked on the door. 'Will,' he said quietly.

The bolts were pulled back softly and the door opened the barest crack before opening just enough for them to be admitted.

'Laurence! Come in, come in.' After taking a quick look down the alley, the door closed behind them and they were inside. 'Pardon, but I did not want anyone who might be watching to see you come in.'

'Are you being watched?'

'One never knows. You can't be too careful. There

are many British agents in Paris, as well you know since you were at one time one of them. There are also agents of the Paris Commune watching us as we watch them. It's a dangerous business. Many houses have been entered and searched by the National Guard, the inhabitants taken away. It is a time when people have to look to themselves, with eyes at the back and front of them, a time when patriotism cannot be taken for granted. It has to be proved—often in the most brutal manner.'

'Then I can only hope we can complete the business we are here for and leave immediately. Every hour that we are here increases the danger.'

The house, overshadowed by others in the grim alley, was dark, with just a few candles flickering in sconces on the walls to lighten the gloom.

'Are any of the others here?' Laurence asked.

'No. We have the house to ourselves for the time being. Two of them have gone down to the south— Marseilles, I think. One can never be sure in this business.' He laughed heartily and clapped Laurence on the shoulder. 'I'm beginning to regret not becoming a soldier, Laurence, so I could inscribe my name in glory, if I felt so inclined, instead of this underworld I inhabit on a daily basis. I'm looking forward to the day when I can return to my home in Warwickshire, marry the lady of my choice and idle my time away in retirement.' He smiled at Delphine, his eyes twinkling. 'Aren't you going to introduce me to your lady wife, Laurence—at least I assume she is your wife?'

Delphine smiled as Laurence introduced them, noting that William Faulkner was fair, quite handsome in a rakish kind of way and that he bowed over her hand with exaggerated courtesy.

'I'm happy to meet you. I suppose my friend has been completely neglectful of telling you anything about me.'

Delphine glanced at her husband with wide-eyed uncertainty. 'I'm afraid he has.'

'You must forgive him. As ever he will have much on his mind. I trust the journey wasn't too taxing.'

'It could have been worse,' Laurence replied. 'It's good of you to go to all this trouble, Will. We are grateful—although I doubt your superiors in the government would see it that way.'

'It's what I do, how I earn my living. The government gets plenty out of me—out of all of us. I make a point of knowing what is going on in most of the prisons in Paris—the Conciergerie in particular, since I spent most of the time you were in there trying to get you out. In the end I hear it was a charming young lady who is now your wife who succeeded where your friends failed,' he said, winking at Delphine. 'I must congratulate you, Lady Beaumont. It was a brave thing you did. Which is just one of the reasons why I'm glad to help in any way I can.'

'What is happening in Paris, Will?'

'Much the same as when you left, I imagine. Arrests are countless. There is a madness in the people, their tempers so inflamed that it is dangerous to open one's mouth lest it be misconstrued.' His expression became serious. 'You have come in time,' he said, his gaze settling on Delphine.

'In time?' Laurence asked. 'What are you talking about, Will?'

'Henri St Clair is to be tried tomorrow. Unless something can be done, his death is a foregone conclusion.'

Delphine's voice shuddered up from the depths of an unutterable horror. 'No,' she whispered. 'Dear God, no.' She moved closer to Will. 'What can be done to save him? Is there anything? A lawyer, perhaps.'

'It cannot be done, Delphine—if I may be so bold as to address you as such. I doubt we could find anyone to defend him in such a short space of time. Besides, it's most unlikely that the Citizen Prosecutor and the jurors would listen. You can witness the trials if you wish to attend. They are open to spectators.'

'Then, yes, I will go to the trial.'

'Will you see him—speak to him?'

'After the trial—I must.'

'We will go together,' Will said. 'I would advise you to stay here, Laurence. There is the danger that someone will recognise you at the Conciergerie.'

'Yes,' Delphine said, looking at her husband. 'You must stay away. I could not bear it if you were taken again.'

Walking towards the Conciergerie took Delphine back to the time when she had come to secure Laurence's release. She was nervous, looking at the faces of those she passed to see if they posed a threat. Laurence was waiting for her back at the house. Even though she couldn't see him she took comfort from that. When they reached the Conciergerie a man stepped out of the entrance in front of her. There was a look in his eyes—an intensity—that ordinarily would have frightened her, but she was beyond fear now. Her one thought was to see her father. She would not be stopped.

The reeking stench of decay inside the Conciergerie was indescribable. People were milling about all over the place, most of them having come to attend the trials and to witness the downfall of more aristocrats. When the proceedings began, Delphine's nerves were strung tight. The prisoners entered slowly, their fear-filled eyes darting around, knowing there would be no mercy at this court. Then she saw her father. Standing by Will's side she took a step back so he would not see her—to do so now would upset him and she wanted to save him more suffering. He would not want her to see his degradation at the hands of the Citizen Prosecutor and the jurors.

He shuffled in behind a long line of prisoners, men and women. Her hand went to her mouth to stifle a sob. She was stunned by his appearance, seeing with her own eyes what his imprisonment had done to him. Once an upright, sprightly man, he was terribly thin, with the pallor of someone who hasn't seen daylight for a long time. Deprivation and hunger and despair and fear had left their mark on him and a sadness that was impossible to hide.

Pity moved her as she watched one prisoner after another sentenced to death, the reason being the fact that they had been born into the nobility. Henri St Clair was no exception. There was not a trace of human sympathy among those doing the sentencing. The trial was indeed a foregone conclusion—even though he had not taken up arms against France and had oppressed no one, the fact that he was an aristo- crat of aristocratic descent automatically made him an enemy of the State.

When he was sentenced to death within twenty- four hours, Delphine caught her breath. Her hand was at her throat, then at her mouth as though to keep in the sound which was surely about to erupt. Will caught her other hand and held it. Quickly they left the court as the prisoners were led away.

'The prisoners will be taken to a common cell to await the time for them to be taken. You can see and speak to your father if you wish, Delphine?'

'Yes,' she whispered. 'I think I must.'

The place where the condemned prisoners were kept was filled to overflowing, the stench of un- washed bodies overwhelming. Seeing her father seated on a chair against the wall with his eyes closed, she called out to him. Looking up, he caught her eye and she felt her heart lurch when he got up and ap- proached at a steady pace, unaware that she was hold- ing her breath and almost choking on the tears that clogged her throat. When he looked at her, the lines in his face deepened. His once thick mane of white hair had thinned, the long white strands hanging down past his ears. He moved slowly, limping, shuffling and awkward.

'Papa,' she whispered, thrusting her hands through the bars.

Surprised by her sudden appearance, he stopped short. Out of a lined, gaunt face his fading, piercing eyes settled on her face. An uncertain smile quivered for a moment on his thin lips, which faded, as if a curtain had been drawn across by some invisible hand and he looked at Delphine with sudden disquiet.

'Delphine?' he queried. He said her name softly, his hoarse voice lingering over it.

She stood frozen in place, her eyes roving lovingly over the man as if he were an apparition she was afraid would vanish if she moved. 'Yes, Papa. It is your Delphine,' she said, feeling Will's quiet, supportive presence behind her.

'This was not the way I expected us to meet again. But—what are you doing here? You should not be. Did you—were you...?'

'Yes,' she said, taking one of his thin hands in her own, her eyes filled with love and consolation. 'I was there. I know, Papa. I heard.'

'My darling girl,' he whispered. 'Tell me, how do you fare? Are you well—with your grandfather?'

She nodded through the tears that swam in her eyes. 'Yes—yes, we are well,' she replied, deciding it best to keep her grandfather's demise from him at this terrible time. 'I—I am wed, now, Papa—to a good man.' His eyes moved to the man behind her. 'This is William Faulkner—a good friend. My husband is Laurence Beaumont. It is too dangerous for him to come here—he, too, was a prisoner not so long ago in the Conciergerie. He saw you on occasion and spoke to you. It was not until our wedding day that he knew of the connection. You might remember him.'

'Yes—yes, I might. But you must go now, my darling—see, the gaoler is moving us on. This is no place for you. You must go with my blessing and my love.'

Delphine could see the gaoler shoving the prisoners into another cell, but she held on to her father's hand until the last. 'Papa,' she murmured, all her anguish in that one word. 'I have been searching for you ever since that terrible day when my aunt and uncle were taken and…' Finding it difficult to recount what had happened to them, she bit her quivering lip and then said, 'I knew you were still alive, that one day I would find you, Papa.'

The cherished title was like a tender caress softly soothing him and tears welled up in his tired eyes as he reached out and caressed her cheek and sighed the words, 'Delphine. *Ma petite* Delphine. My dear child. Go now.' He looked at Will, who stepped forward and drew her away.

Delphine watched him being taken away by the gaoler and not until she could no longer see him did she turn and let Will lead her outside. There was a man in the doorway, directing those who had been to watch the trial of the condemned. Vaguely her mind registered his identity, the black beard and intense gaze. Gaspard Ducat. He looked at her and then turned away. Had he recognised her? She didn't know.

All she knew at that moment was that she couldn't bear it. A kind of despair entered her then, recognition of the possibility of failure. She wanted to put her head down and weep.

They made their way back to the house in silence. Delphine wanted to scream and shout to the world the injustice of it all, but wretched and stricken as she was, she was also strong, and with this strength came the same determination that had carried her through her dangerous assignments in the past. Whatever the cost, she must save her beloved father from his sentence, to uphold him at this time.

Chapter Thirteen

The moment Laurence saw Delphine's face, knowing her misery, his whole body leaned towards her in a yearning to protect her from grief, from harm. His arms went round her and he held her, this woman who had become so beloved. She was brave and spirited, and to see that brave spirit battered and bruised in her hurt and concern for her father tore at his heart.

Taking her face between his hands, he watched as her tears like crystal raindrops spilled from her eyes and she began to cry, her face awash, not speaking as she gave way to an outpouring of emotion. He wrapped his strong arms about her once more, and not until her sobbing eased did he gently hold her away from him.

'Tell me,' he said. 'You saw your father?'

As her tears subsided and her body became still, she tilted her head back, looked at him and nodded, swallowing down what remained of her tears. 'After he was sentenced.'

'How was he? How did he look?'

'Physically he is very weak,' she said, wiping the remaining tears from her cheeks with the back of her hand. 'Mentally I would say he is unimpaired. But it's not fair,' she cried. 'It's just not fair. How can this happen? So many were tried at the same time—all of them condemned to death. No one was spared.'

'I know, Delphine. It's not fair. None of it is fair.'

'I'm devastated, Laurence. I cannot see him die. I must get him back somehow.'

'It will be difficult,' Will said. 'Guards are nearly always present and doors to the cells are locked and barred. I know well from repeated investigation how escape-proof the prisons in Paris are.'

'Not quite,' Laurence countered. 'I am proof that escape is possible.'

'When I was at the Conciergerie I saw Citizen Ducat—Gaspard Ducat,' Delphine told them. 'He might help us—as he did before. I understand that the only way left is to buy his safety—as we did for you, Laurence. Do you think he can be persuaded to do the same for my father?'

Laurence looked at Will. 'What do you think, Will?'

With a furrowed brow, Will stood in thoughtful silence. 'I know the man Ducat. He is known to us and has been useful to us in the past—for a price. Before he became a guard he was a professional thief. There wasn't a house in Paris he couldn't rifle if he had a mind—not a watch, a snuffbox or a priceless necklace he couldn't steal. He can claim the monopoly where escapees are concerned, but corruption among the guards is rife. The place is full of aristocrats, all eager to pay for any kind of privilege that will make their lives more comfortable.'

'Then why don't they pay the guards to help them escape—as we did for Laurence?'

'Because they are not all like Citizen Ducat, who has grown fat on bribes. They are not prepared to take the risk. However, I believe it can be done—if we don't run out of time.'

'Before they come to take him away,' Delphine whispered. 'I would never forgive myself if I did not try to rescue him.'

'I will see what can be done,' Will said.

Laurence was alert. 'What have you in mind?'

Gravely, unsmilingly, Will looked back at his friend. 'To have a word with Citizen Ducat. I believe we can trust him. I wouldn't be taking the risk if I had any doubts. Were your father still in his cell it would be less trouble getting him out. Now he is with the condemned in the holding room it will be difficult separating him from the others without arousing suspicion—unless…'

'Unless we can fake his death,' Laurence said, having read Will's expression correctly and knowing it was a method often used in the past to get political prisoners out of various prisons in Paris.

A moment's silence followed those terrible words and each one echoed solemnly in their hearts and conscience.

Will nodded. 'It is our only hope.'

Delphine felt her heart contract. 'But—how can that be done?'

Will produced a small bottle from his pocket. 'Laudanum—a tincture of opium. There is enough in this bottle to induce a deep sleep. If we can persuade Ducat to play his part, Henri St Clair will be declared dead shortly after it has been administered.'

Alarm gripped Delphine. 'But—he is not well. Might such a strong dose not prove fatal?'

'I hope not,' Will said, his expression sympathetic. 'But it is our only chance of getting him out of there.' He looked at Laurence. 'What do you think?'

Laurence nodded. 'You are right. It is our only chance.'

'You—you mean to bring my father out in a coffin?' Delphine could not bear the thought of it. It was too horrendous for words.

'He won't know anything about it,' Laurence said gently. 'He'll be asleep, I promise you.'

Logic and reason, so long the hallmark of Delphine's character in the past when faced with difficulties, fled in an instant. Clinging to the last vestiges of hope and refusing to admit defeat, she nodded. 'Yes—then that is what we must do.'

'I have money to pay Ducat.'

Will looked at Laurence. 'He will want a tidy sum.'

'Of course he will. I have come prepared.'

Delphine stared at her husband in amazement. 'You have?'

'I am not entirely penniless, Delphine. I do still have funds at my disposal and I cannot think of a more worthy cause.'

* * *

When Will returned from the Conciergerie, telling them that Ducat would carry out the plan immediately and he was to return to the Conciergerie in one hour—already some of the condemned were being taken away in the tumbrils—Laurence disappeared up the rickety stairs.

When he came back down a few minutes later he was unrecognisable. He was dressed in a dirty smock and baggy hose which hung in wrinkled folds round his long, well-muscled legs. He had greased his dark hair which stuck out from beneath a shapeless cap pulled down over his ears and walked with a stoop to disguise his height.

Delphine had to put her hand to her mouth to stifle a giggle, while Will looked him up and down with a critical eye.

'For the love of God, my dear friend, if you are to drive the cart to the Conciergerie then try to keep your eyes down when you run across any guards—and don't run them through with that glare of yours lest they incarcerate you yet again.'

Laurence gave a reluctant grin. 'I'll do my best, but it will be difficult, Will—the sight of those guards who show the prisoners no mercy makes my blood boil.'

'You must try to ignore them. Our quest will not take long.'

Laurence's disguise had relaxed Delphine's high-strung nerves a little. It added a note of humour to this strange and precipitate flight of theirs. She took a deep breath, as if she had just surfaced after swimming for a long time under water. After all the days of doubt and anxiety, William Faulkner's quiet confidence left her feeling hopeful and what a comfort he was.

As if by magic, Will had acquired a cart from somewhere.

At the door Laurence looked down at her. His expression was grim and a touch apprehensive. Delphine stood facing him, taking judicious note of the rigid set of his jaw and feeling a tendril of fear coil in the pit of her stomach.

'You will be careful?' she whispered anxiously, placing her hand on his arm.

'We'll be back with your father before you know it. Wait here, Delphine. If everything goes to plan, we will soon be on our way to Calais.' He left her then, every muscle tensed and ready to act.

Before Delphine could utter a word, the two men were on their way. Taut with apprehension, she waited, aware that if they did not succeed then nothing could save them. If anything went wrong with the escape, a hue and cry would follow and they would all be arrested. God help us, she thought, and for the first time in a long time she began to pray, fervently beseeching Him to take pity on her father and allow him to be returned to her.

Hearing the rumble of wheels on the cobbles outside the house jerked her out of her silent vigil and she flew to the door and flung it open. The two men leaped off the wagon. After glancing up and down the alley to make sure they were quite alone, they went to the back of the wagon and pulled out a crude wooden box, then between them carried it into the house.

With a cry, Delphine fell to her knees beside it while Laurence prised the slats apart. Her father lay fast asleep—so deep was his slumber that only the slight movement of his chest told them he was alive. She looked at Laurence.

'Did everything go to plan? Was anyone suspicious?'

He shook his head. 'Nothing about your father's assumed death struck the other condemned or the guards as being at all unusual or abnormal. Death is a frequent occurrence among the inhabitants of the Conciergerie. Everyone is used to it and thinks only of their own incarceration and if they will get away with their heads intact.'

'Did you see Citizen Ducat?'

'I did.'

'And? Did he recognise you?'

Laurence nodded. 'He did, but we did not exchange a word. He has his money. That's all he cared about.'

'What now?'

'We place your father somewhere more comfortable and wait until he wakes up. After a change of clothes and some food inside him, we'll be on our way. With any luck we'll pass through the gates without being apprehended.'

They stretched him out on the sofa, but nothing could dispel the deep slumber into which Henri St Clair had fallen.

* * *

When he finally awoke night had fallen on the city of Paris and it was too late for them to leave. Henri was confused on waking, unable to take in what had happened to him and where he was, until Delphine leaned over him and placed a kiss on his forehead.

'Don't be alarmed, Papa. You're safe now.'

He raised his head slowly and looked around, finally settling his watery gaze on her face without betraying the slightest sign of surprise. 'Where—who…?' He spoke softly, in a voice which sounded something like a dream. Then, after a moment during which Delphine could hear her heart hammering, he closed his eyes once more. 'I'm so very tired.'

Delphine's heart ached with sympathy. Was he so weak that words meant nothing to him? She tried again. 'Father, it's me, Delphine.'

'Delphine—yes, yes.' He looked at her, staring through her as if she were transparent. His head sank back and he closed his eyes.

'We managed to get you out of the Conciergerie, Papa. When the city wakes we will leave Paris and head for Calais, where we will take ship for England.'

He looked at her dazedly once more. 'England? But—how did I get out? I remember feeling tired—after I was given something to drink… I cannot recall anything after that.'

'We'll explain everything to you later. But now you must sleep and when you wake you must eat something. We have a long journey ahead of us.'

'I dreamt that some day I would be free, but I never thought it would happen.'

Again he closed his eyes. Delphine's heart was too full to do more than murmur, 'He knows me and yet he seems so far away.'

'He's been incarcerated for a long time—in isolation for most of it. He's also still suffering the effects of the laudanum. It will wear off,' Laurence said softly, placing a comforting arm about her shoulders. 'We'll make him comfortable and let him sleep.' He hugged her close. 'Are you all right, Delphine? This is difficult for you, I know.'

'Yes, yes, it is. From the moment I saw him in the Conciergerie I became completely undone. My father was there, a living, breathing remembrance of my life in France. He'd always been there for me and then he was lost. And now here he is in the flesh. But when I remember those poor people, some whose lives will already have ended, I have much to be thankful for.'

Delphine didn't leave her father for a moment. Gone was the upright man who'd once had so much energy and a passion for life. Now he looked broken sitting there, broken and old and lost, and yet, at sixty years of age, he was not old in years. There was only the barest hint of the man he had been.

For the return journey to Calais they swapped the coach for a more sturdy, closed conveyance, the better to conceal the occupants. Will, with nothing better to do for the time being, offered to go with them, acting as their driver.

'We cannot expect that of you,' Delphine said. 'It is too generous. I should hate anything to happen to you on our account.'

Will grinned. 'It's the least I can do. Your husband has helped me out of many a scrape. It's payback time. I shall make sure to look and act the part of your coachman.'

'As agents for the Crown, Delphine,' her husband informed her, 'we are adept at making ourselves invisible, using any disguise to blend in with any situation so our presence doesn't arouse suspicion—as you witnessed when I changed to go to the Conciergerie.' He slapped his friend on the back good-naturedly. 'Thank you, Will. I appreciate this.'

'Think nothing of it. It will be a relief to get out of Paris for a bit.'

The following morning they left the house and headed for the gate. Delphine's father, still sleeping off the effects of the drug, sat propped in a corner of the coach, his head resting on a cushion. Delphine's heart was in her mouth and she was holding her breath as they neared the gate. It was thronged with people passing through, some carriages and produce stopped and prodded by the guards—citizen soldiers of the Republic—for aristocrats were still trying to flee in various disguises. Delphine had never known the kind of fear that gripped her then. This was a fear of the unknown, a false word, a lost moment of time and the hope of safety with it.

Taking the papers Laurence produced—four

English subjects heading for Calais—when they were handed back, Laurence said, *'Merci, Citizen,'* amiably. He spoke with an exaggerated English accent. This seemed to amuse some of the men standing about. With laughter and grumbles and curses from some, and comments on the *meddlesome Anglaise*, it was an immense relief for Delphine to leave Paris behind, which before they had passed through the gate had seemed unlikely to free them alive.

Their journey towards the coast was more fraught than their journey to Paris. The guards on the gates were more thorough in their inspection of the coach and its occupants. Delphine's blood would freeze in her veins when she realised the peril in which they all stood. Fortunately her father was asleep for most of the time and they did not wake him, which was fortunate for he spoke English with a French accent, which would have aroused the guard's suspicions.

Despite the stoppages in the villages along the way, they made the journey to Calais quickly—a feat they managed to accomplish by the expedient, if reckless and costly method of paying large sums to coaching inns to change the team of horses after fifteen miles or so and travelling at first light and not stopping for the night until dark.

It was hard saying goodbye to Will. Laurence had told her he was a true friend. Will had proved he was that in many ways over the days they had been together. He expected to be returning to England himself very soon. When Laurence asked if he was going to retire from the service, he laughed.

'Paris is infested with spies,' he said. 'One less will not make a difference. I will visit you in Cornwall before too long.'

And so they had parted and were fortunate to find a vessel to take them to Dover within an hour of arriving in Calais. As she stepped on to the boat and watched the French coast recede into the distance, never to return, Delphine thought of how much of her past was buried there with her murdered family, whom she had loved. That was past. Her future was with Laurence and her father.

On reaching Dover they began to relax. Their flight was over, their mission accomplished. Henri St Clair was unsure of many things. After watching as the chateau which had been the home of St Clairs for many decades was burned to the ground and his brother and his wife executed, he had felt his own life was over. He seemed to occupy some private place within his head from which everyone else was excluded.

'Do you think he will improve?,' Delphine asked her anxious husband, whose anxiety did she but know was for her and not her father.

'He will when he's settled. We'll leave for Cornwall as soon as I get things tied up in London. The sea air will act as a tonic.'

Henri spoke little on the journey and only pecked at his food when they stopped for refreshment.

* * *

On reaching London, Delphine began to see a lightening of his spirit. Glancing out of the window, his eyes fell on some street sellers. He noticed one of them selling brightly coloured ribbons and lace and all kinds of bric-a-brac.

'See the colours, Delphine,' he said, a note of excitement in his voice. 'What would you like?'

She laughed. 'A red ribbon, Papa. You used to tell me you would buy me a red ribbon to tie up my golden hair.'

Staring at her, he seemed to reflect for a moment and then a smile appeared on his lips as a memory slipped into his head. 'So I did. I remember. And you shall have them. I will buy you a whole bunch of red ribbons when I can.'

It was a relief to be back in London. Delphine was disappointed to find that Julia had returned home, but she had left a letter for Laurence informing him that she would return shortly when her husband came to negotiate the sale of the house. Delphine settled her father in his own room, where he spent most of his time for the first two weeks, either sleeping or sitting by the window with a book or a newspaper open in front of him.

For the first time since leaving for Paris, Laurence and Delphine found time for themselves.

Entering his wife's room after spending a little time with her father, who had surprised him by agreeing to play a game of chess, a game which had entertained Henri for an hour or so before he became tired, he found Delphine seated at her dressing table in her nightdress, brushing her hair. Laurence studied her, thinking there was something different about her, that she looked different somehow. Her cheeks were flushed, rounder. His gaze strayed to the contours of her breasts pushed up from the bodice of her nightdress. They seemed rounder, fuller. On the whole she seemed remarkably relaxed and content. Could this be the result of having her father back in her life— or something else?

Going to her, he settled his hand on her shoulders and placed a kiss in the hollow of her neck before meeting her eyes in the mirror. 'We have spent all our time together since leaving London for Paris and yet I have missed you—we have had much on our minds for too long.' He smiled at her. 'I have to say marriage suits you,' he remarked huskily. 'You are positively blooming with good health. If I didn't know better, I would say our marriage bed has proved fruitful.'

His words, spoken with unsuspecting lightness, seemed to jolt Delphine out of her languor and her eyes snapped open, locking on to his. For what seemed to be an eternity they remained so, neither of them moving and scarcely breathing. Although there was the noise of passing carriages in the street, there was stillness and silence about them.

Laurence broke the spell. 'You are, aren't you, Delphine?'

'What?'

'With child?'

'Yes,' she whispered. 'At least, I believe I am. I think I conceived that day at the cove.'

Taking her hand, he raised her up and touched her face, then cradled her cheek, then he kissed her and there was a trembling deep inside him. The scent of her, the taste of her mouth overwhelmed him. It felt as if the endless days of their journey fell away in seconds.

Releasing her, Laurence quickly began removing his clothes while his wife stood in silent fascination, watching him. Without words or questions and with the infinite patience of a true lover, slowly and gently he slipped her nightdress from her shoulders, sighing over every inch of flesh as it became exposed and placing tantalising kisses here and there before he laid her on the bed.

Raising his arms on either side of her, he leaned over her, his eyes caressing every curve of her body, expressing his delight in the gentle curve of her belly where their child was growing.

'You are so beautiful,' he murmured, lowering his body to hers, 'more so now that you are with child.' He sighed deeply. 'I love you so much, Delphine. Have I told you that before?'

'No—I have been waiting for you to do so.'

'There were times when you came to London that I thought I would go mad with wanting you. When you berated me so severely for deceiving you I was afraid you hated me.'

'Laurence, I'm sorry. I never hated you. It's been a trying time for both of us.'

'It wasn't easy keeping what I knew from you, but I was not prepared to put you at risk. I couldn't bear the thought that anything might happen to you—that I might lose you. I would do anything to protect you.' He gazed into the amber depths of her eyes. 'I may accuse you of being a siren, a vixen, a hoyden, even— but as long as you stay yourself beneath it all then I am well satisfied. I've no desire to change you— you are the most unconventional young woman I've known, my love, so don't start now. You mean everything to me. You are my life.' Sighing, he brushed the backs of his fingers gently over her cheek. 'I love you, Delphine. I love you so much it hurts.'

'And I love you, my darling. So very much. But the troubles are over for us now, thank God, and we can begin our lives as husband and wife at last. We have all the time in the world now we are home, so let's take advantage of it.'

Reaching up to brush his lips with a kiss, Delphine let her hands slide up over his chest, a finger tracing the line of his strong jaw, coming to rest on the scar on his eyelid.

'How did you come by that scar? Who were you fighting?'

'No one. I fell off my horse when I was a boy. Mary challenged me to a race. I was showing off, thinking I could beat her.'

'And did you?'

He chuckled low in his throat. 'No. I fell off, hitting my head. I recall my sister laughing, telling me not to be so arrogant in future by thinking I could beat her. I was so humiliated at the time. It did nothing for my pride—letting my sister best me on a horse—and my ego took a battering.'

'Poor you,' she whispered, placing her lips on the scar and kissing it gently.

His mouth touched hers again, at first demanding, then sweet and achingly tender. She closed her eyes in rapture and her neck arched backwards when she felt his lips on her breasts. Giving herself up to total abandon and revelling in the pleasure he was giving her as his lips kissed the smooth swell of her abdomen, his long, lean fingers holding her waist, pausing now and then to murmur intimate, sensual endearments, she moaned, her emotions soaring even higher, her excitement for what was to happen next uncontrollable, and she wanted him to take her immediately.

Once again Laurence showed her the true meaning of sensuality and passion. A husky moan escaped her and with her heartbeat throbbing in her ears, her blood flowing through her veins like a liquid flame as he drew out all her suppressed longings that surpassed all the other times they had made love, it was far more profound and she could deny him nothing.

In the glowing aftermath of their loving they lay for a precious moment in one another's arms. With their limbs entwined they were oblivious to the world outside, only the sound of their breathing disturbing the silence of the room. Turning towards her, Laurence stroked her hair streaming over his shoulder in a mass of contrasting shadows, his lips brushing her warmly flushed cheek. She lay as one drugged in his arms, arms that she knew were gentle and tender, and would never let her go. Rousing herself from the delicious torpor that enfolded her, she sighed, her eyes fluttering open.

Laurence smiled and his rather grave face softened with tenderness. 'I wonder why you fire my blood as no other woman has done, my love. I fear I am quite besotted with desire for you. What is your secret?' he murmured. 'I swear you are a temptress, a witch, out to entrap me.'

Her smile was sublime as she reached up and traced his cheeks with the tips of her fingers. 'There is no secret, Laurence. I am neither witch nor temptress. I am me—myself.'

Taking her hand, he placed his lips in her palm. 'And a rare creature you are, Delphine, an incomparable, precious being who has this new life on the way, the woman who is to bear my child.'

'I want our baby to be born at Pendene, Laurence. You will make that possible?'

'Absolutely. As soon as I have seen to the sale of the house we will leave London.'

On a sigh she snuggled against him, loving the feel of his arms about her, his warmth. 'Thank you. I never did thank you, did I?'

'For what?'

'Doing what you do for my father—helping me to deal with everything.'

'He's your father. How could I not?'

'Everything seems to be in such a muddle. I'll be glad when we get to Cornwall. I don't think I like London very much. But when we get to Pendene—will everything work out—with the mine and everything?'

A worried expression stole over Laurence's face. 'I hope so. I sincerely intend working at it. I can't pretend it will be easy—capital is going to be a problem, but one way or another I will make a decent home for all of us.'

Delphine slipped her arm about his waist, placing her head against his chest where his heart was beating furiously. 'Of course you will—we will. We will do it together, Laurence.'

When they settled down to sleep, as she closed her eyes she felt as if she were walking on air and a smile settled on her lips, a smile that told her she loved him—and, oh, yes, love him she did, with her whole heart. This she did not deny.

Gradually Henri began to improve. He enjoyed walking in the garden and taking the occasional carriage ride in the park with Delphine. The deep sadness and heaviness had lifted from his face and he bore himself straighter. The shock of their meeting over, Delphine was beginning to see him more as he had been, hopeful and touched with a jaunty gallantry.

It was on one of their walks in the garden that she told him of the child she was expecting and the work she had been involved in while she searched for news of him in France. 'I refused to accept that you were dead.'

He listened carefully, deeply moved and angry because of what she had put herself through.

'I am sorry, Delphine. It has been a terrible time for you, too. We can never go back to France now. You do understand that?'

'We are the lucky ones,' Delphine said and he nodded.

'How fragile life is, how fragile we are.'

'Yes, we are, Papa. But this is the beginning and end of everything we knew.'

'When I last saw you, you were a girl—my little Delphine. Now you are a woman with the heart of a lion. Much of the St Clair blood is carried in you. You bear the old France in you—and the new France, when the violence ends. You must live your life with pride and with courage—like your ancestors before you. Sadly I cannot give you a title—those things are done with.'

Dinner two weeks after their return to London was a particularly joyous affair. Sir Godfrey was to dine with them and Delphine's father surprised them by telling them he would join them. The table shone with silver and crystal ware and gilt-framed paintings of family and hunting scenes adorned the walls.

Looking particularly regal in a gown of saffron silk shot with green and her hair immaculately coiffed, Delphine and Laurence presided over this, the first dinner they had given since their marriage. Relieved to see her father looking at ease and joining in the conversation occasionally, Delphine relaxed.

As the meal progressed, with discussion about the troubles in France and the British stance now the two countries were at war, the conversation turned to more pleasant matters in Cornwall, Pendene in particular. When Sir Godfrey questioned Laurence about the mine, becoming caught up in his enthusiasm, Sir Godfrey's interest deepened.

'It has potential, you say?'

'According to the experts I brought in it would appear so. There is a vein of copper they tell me that would be rich and profitable—and new seams to be opened. The problem is that it needs capital—the amount of which I do not have. I am negotiating with the banks to raise the capital. If they sanction the loan and with some of the capital that will come from selling the house, then I intend to install a new steam engine and sink another shaft, to open up the levels. When it starts producing, the mine should pay for itself.'

'In order to help you I am willing to invest money in the mine.'

Laurence was taken aback. 'You would?'

Sir Godfrey smiled. 'I have every faith in both you and your mine, Laurence, and it will give me immense pleasure seeing my investment grow.'

'I thank you for your offer, Sir Godfrey. It is a little complicated at present, but I am sure that it will be a good investment long term, even if the yields are not all that they might be at present.'

'Nevertheless, I am willing to take the risk after I have studied the facts and figures.'

'What I suggest is that you go and see my lawyer and ask him to advise you further. If you decide to go ahead with the investment—and I sincerely hope you will—because I am already his client, you will have to ask your own lawyer to act on your behalf if necessary.'

'I, too, might be interested in investing in your mine, Laurence,' Henri said, having listened to the discussion about the mine with interest. 'After all, you are married to my daughter and any offspring— one of which will be born in the near future, which has made me a very happy man—will benefit from my investment.'

Delphine stared at him. 'But—how can you do that, Papa? You lost everything in France.'

'Not entirely. Fearing what would happen in France, I transferred funds from Tellson's Bank in Paris to the London branch in Temple Bar. I wondered if I was doing the right thing at the time. It appears I was.'

'And you can access the funds?'

'I sincerely hope so. Tellson's Bank has served me well—and other aristocrats in France. I was assured it would extend the same courtesy to me in London.'

'Goodness!' Delphine said, a happy smile on her lips. 'I don't know what to say. I certainly wasn't expecting this.'

'How could you? Nothing is the same any more. When I was in the Conciergerie I was reaching the point of total despair. Now there has been a huge change to my life and I am at times confused, but I will try not to let the thoughts that still trouble me override the positive ones. So be happy, Delphine, at what I am offering.' He smiled. 'So you see, *ma petite* Delphine, I will be able to afford your red ribbons after all.'

With tears in her eyes, Delphine went to him and embraced him. 'Thank you, Papa. I love you.'

Laurence was clearly moved by what these two men were offering him. 'It is impossible to describe my feeling at this time except to say that I am indeed grateful to you both. Your offers are generous in the extreme. I will try not to let you down. The mine will be the best run mine in Cornwall.'

During their absence, Pendene had been put into good order. Milly McGuire, along with Agatha and her husband, who had come to Pendene from Tregannon on the death of Delphine's grandfather, had worked wonders with the house and gardens. They had been tended, pruned, planted and nurtured by men John had brought in, bringing them back to their former glory.

Delphine had worried how her father would settle in to a life in Cornwall. But even with the effects of prison and the flight from his beloved France still on him, knowing that this was how it had to be, he began to gather up the threads of life and his affairs with a boldness and purpose and confidence that Delphine and Laurence could not help but admire. It was evident to all that Henri St Clair was no fool, but a man who combined the results of good birth and character, a man willing to take a risk and had no illusions.

On the day when Delphine and Laurence walked to Tregannon, the sky was blue above them with slowly moving clouds. The sound of gulls swirling and screeching over the cliffs disturbed the silence that hung about the old house. When they were close Delphine paused and looked at it, her heart stirring painfully for it contained so much of herself. Knowing her grandfather would not be inside to welcome her, she was reluctant to enter.

As they walked to the door, an ache for the past and her lost family came to her. A lump rose in her throat when she entered and felt the emptiness of the house wrap itself around her, a house which had once pulsated with the lives of those who had lived in it. An eerie, haunting silence shrouded the interior, with an unearthly quiet which struck deep into Delphine's heart. Slowly she went from room to room, trailing her fingers over the familiar furniture, lingering a while longer on the chair her grandfather had favoured close to the hearth.

'What are you thinking?' Laurence asked, watching her closely.

'I'm thinking of my grandfather and my mother. I miss them both—and Aunt Amelia. Everyone I have loved has been taken from me.'

'You still have your father.'

'Yes, and I thank God for him. I almost lost him also.' She sighed, looking out of the window over the garden, which John had kept carefully tended. 'What shall we do with it, Laurence? It can't remain empty. It needs a family to bring it back to life, for laughter and joy to ring within its walls—as it did when I was a child.'

Moving to stand behind her, Laurence put his arms about her and held her close. 'It's early days, Delphine. We'll have to give it careful thought. There's no hurry.'

Deeply affected by what she had seen and the painful images and memories it had evoked, Delphine sighed. 'Yes, you're right. I couldn't bear to think of just anyone living here.'

Delphine settled down to life at Pendene with ease, and for Laurence life with Delphine was everything he ever hoped it could be and more. A surge of tenderness and profound pride swept through him at her sweetness and candour, and she filled him with joyous contentment. She was indeed a rare woman and everything he had ever wanted. He loved her, all of her—her intelligence, her sensitivity, her gentle, passionate nature—but most of all he loved her courage, the kind of courage that had enabled her to confront adversity time after time.

When her labour began suddenly and fiercely one day while strolling outside in the cold winter air, with dawning alarm Laurence gathered her into his arms and mounted the stairs and carried his tender burden to their room. Everything was blotted from her mind, the centre of her being focusing only on getting the baby out as soon as possible.

With the birth of the child, a boy, the relief was enormous. Holding her son—a large baby, yet as soft and light as thistledown—she looked sleepily at Laurence, who had come into the bedroom and was leaning over her.

'We have a beautiful son,' she whispered. 'A beautiful, perfectly formed son.'

His eyes glittering with unsuppressed pride and joy, Laurence smoothed the curls off her cheek stained with a rosy blush. His sensual lips quirked in a half-smile. 'A son. How wonderful is that? He is beautiful—just like his mother,' he said, his voice raw from the emotion of the past few hours.

Knowing how hazardous childbirth could often be, Laurence had lived the horrors of the things that could go wrong. Leaning forward, he covered her mouth with his own, the gentle kiss eloquent of the profound love he felt for her and relief that her ordeal was over and she was well.

'Thank you, my love,' he breathed against her lips.

Setting her cheek against the tiny head in her arms, Delphine closed her eyes and whispered, 'You're welcome, my love.'

Epilogue

1795

Things were going well for Laurence. After all his determination and hard work, the mine was up and working and he and the two shareholders were beginning to reap the rewards. The mine was producing copper, working steadily and began showing a profit sooner than Laurence had expected. They were mining seams that were accessible and planning to mine even deeper. A large number of miners looking for work were employed from nearby villages and hamlets, miners who had been out of work for a long time and suffered hardship and hunger. Laurence felt that they were custodians of the present and creating something for the future.

It was summertime and visitors arrived at Pendene. Laurence's sisters had travelled down to spend several weeks by the sea without their husbands, bringing the children. Mary had brought her two darling little girls, Caroline and Mary, and Julia her daughter Charlotte.

The day could not have been more perfect a summer's day. The clear blue sky and the gentle breeze stirred the trees and flowers that grew in profusion in the gardens surrounding the house and the air was heady with their scents. Attired in a gown of lavender and lace trim, Delphine walked beside Laurence on the path along the edge of the lawn, linking her arm through his. It was a joyous time for everyone. When they gathered together on the terrace after dinner, they talked desultorily about a variety of things, with much reminiscing and remembering of family and friends, past and present.

Delphine's eyes drifted towards the children, thinking what a charming picture they made, their own Alexander Charles Beaumont toddling on behind the older children with a harassed-looking nursemaid trying to keep control as they played hide and seek, which entailed a great deal of activity and laughter.

Unable to keep up with the girls, Alex flopped down on the grass, his face rosy and smiling, and then he rolled on to his hands and knees and began crawling after Charlotte. He was a beautiful child and he resembled his father in many ways. As young as he was, he even had the same jut to his baby jaw as Laurence, the same scowl, the same green eyes and an air about him of masculine fierceness.

'What are you thinking, Laurence?'

'I was thinking of you and how lucky we are. I knew the moment I laid eyes on you that you were different from any other woman I had known—that you were the one for me.'

Delphine stared at her husband in surprise. 'How could you possibly have known that?'

'Because to me, that day, after being an inmate of one of Paris's most infamous prisons for twelve long months, you were the most beguiling, beautiful person I had seen in a long time. It is a memory I carried with me when we parted on Guernsey. It is a memory that I shall carry with me always.'

Delphine's softly glowing eyes delved into his as she spoke through softly smiling lips. 'And from that day forward there has been no one else for me—or before that. You were the man I had unknowingly longed for—my Prince Charming. Do you actually think we were meant for each other from the beginning?'

Laurence smiled down at her. 'Why not? I had never found ease with any other woman and when you came into my life that day in Paris, it was as if you had stepped out of a dream I had been nurturing all my life. I was smitten—swept away by you, if you like—and I knew I had found the woman of my heart.'

Hearing the gravel crunch behind them they paused, about to turn around when suddenly a familiar voice said, 'Pardon me for intruding on your stroll, but I hope you are pleased to see me.'

They turned simultaneously to find William Faulkner beaming at them, a very pretty young lady by his side.

'Will!' Laurence said, his face breaking into a wide, welcoming smile as he caught his good friend by the shoulders and hugged him. 'You should have told us you were coming. As you see, we have a houseful, but you are most welcome—and your young lady—to stay with us as long as you wish,' he said, releasing Will and focusing his attention on the pretty young woman with strawberry-blonde hair and soft blue eyes. 'Introduce me to your companion, Will.'

'Margaret is my companion, Laurence, and my wife of two months.'

'I hope you will both be very happy.' Laurence kissed Margaret's hand and Delphine was introduced.

'I'm delighted to see you both,' Delphine said, feeling a liking for this young woman immediately. There was a zest about her, a sparkle in the strawberry-blonde curls and blue eyes, which were friendly and, Delphine suspected, often given to mischief. When she got to know her better she would find that she was also discerning and gentlehearted. 'Welcome to Pendene. I second Laurence's invitation. We'd love to have you stay.'

'Thank you,' Margaret said. 'You are very kind and welcoming. We feel though that we must not impose upon you too much.'

'You are not imposing.'

Laurence looked at his friend. 'I heard you were no longer working for the Foreign Office, Will.'

'No. Like you I'd had enough of spying and risking my life in Paris. We are living in Warwickshire at Levisham Park with my parents,' he said, averting his eyes and not enlarging on this, but it was not lost on Laurence, who knew how difficult life had always been for his friend as the youngest of five brothers. 'And you, Laurence. I recall you telling me you had fallen on hard times—although this place is impressive. Things must be on the up.'

'Let's just say that I've been doing what I can to restore the family fortunes rather than deplete them. I spend my days up to my ears in paperwork, trying to turn shillings into pounds. I inherited a defunct copper mine—which, with sound investment from my father-in-law and Sir Godfrey Bucklow, is beginning to show a profit.'

'I'm glad to hear it. How is your father, by the way?' he asked Delphine.

'He is well—in fact, he's living here at Pendene. He misses France, of course, but he will not go back to live in a Republic.'

'I can understand that. I would like to meet him if I may.'

'Come along. I will take you. He has much to thank you for. When we told him how we managed to get him out of the Conciergerie he could not believe it. He still talks of it to anyone who cares to listen.'

Will grinned. 'And who can blame him? It's not every day prisoners get out of that place—only your father and my good friend here.'

The following day, with an idea having formed in both their minds, Laurence and Delphine were taking William and Margaret to see Tregannon. They were walking towards the cove when Laurence told Will and Margaret he had something to show them, something they hoped would change their lives.

'And after that,' Laurence said, 'I have a proposition to put to you.'

Will eyed him sceptically. 'Oh? And what might that be?'

Margaret laughed, which made her curls bounce. 'It all sounds very mysterious, Laurence. What can it be?'

'Be patient,' Delphine told her. 'I think you will like the surprise.'

When they were almost at Tregannon they paused on a low hill and looked at the house ahead of them.

'A house?' Margaret gasped, all astonishment.

'It's Tregannon,' Delphine explained, standing beside her. 'It's my mother's old home—my grandfather lived here until his death two years ago. It was part of my dowry when I married Laurence. It's been empty ever since. It needs living in—a family—but we've always held back, waiting for the right people to move in. I think you and Will are the right people.'

Margaret stared at her, uncomprehending, and then as Delphine's meaning dawned on her, she looked back at the house.

'Come and have a look inside.'

They loved it. They knew nothing about its history. What they saw was a lovely old house, weathered perfectly into the landscape. After a tour of the inside, Margaret's eyes sparkled as she turned to Will.

'Oh, Will, it's perfect. Do you like it?'

He nodded, overcome with emotion. They kissed and hugged. 'We couldn't have chosen better ourselves.'

Delphine and Laurence exchanged satisfied looks.

'There,' Delphine said. 'That's settled then.'

Laurence gave Will a gentle slap on the back. 'I will see to any work that needs to be carried out.'

'You mentioned a proposition, Laurence.'

He nodded. 'John McGuire, in his capacity of estate manager, is leaving. He's stayed on until I can find someone else. I need someone to look after the estate and the staff. You have a business brain, Will. You would be perfect. Since the opening of the mine there is more work, more responsibility, which John doesn't want.'

'What's he doing?'

'Something far more lucrative than managing Pendene—which involves a boat, a crew and frequent trips across to Guernsey in the dead of night.'

Will laughed. 'Ah—well, yes. I think I get the picture. Lucrative, you say. Have you not thought of becoming involved yourself?'

'I confess I did consider it.'

'But?'

'As an outsider and knowing the penalties for smuggling, one has to be naturally cautious. Initially I did consider it when I approached Delphine's grandfather to sell me the land giving me access to the sea.' He laughed. 'Smuggling appealed to my adventuring spirit. I always thought it would provide money to reopen the mine and make some kind of protest against the iniquitous taxation that the government imposes on us.'

'But? What went wrong?'

'Smuggling is against the law, Will. It would not look good for the Master of Pendene to be involved in the trade. It would reflect badly on me. Although,' he said with a grin and a wink, 'I'm not against turning a blind eye when I find a cask of brandy on the doorstep after a run.'

Delphine stood on the edge of the high cliff overlooking the sea. The rocks below plunged down to the beach where the water rippled deep blue in the sun. It was calm, just enough movement for the waves to break lazily on the sand before being sucked back in. She sighed and there was no sadness in that sigh, only sheer pleasure and satisfaction. When someone came to stand beside her she turned expectantly, her eyes gleaming in anticipation.

Laurence smiled lovingly down at her. She wore a gown of apple-green and her golden hair was loose, rising and falling gently in the breeze.

'I thought I would find you here. The sea looks inviting.'

'Doesn't it.'

'How about a swim?'

Delphine turned her head and looked at him. There was a mischievous glint of a promise in his eyes— and something more wicked for later. Her smile was sublime. 'I'm willing if you are?'

'Our favourite cove?'

His eyes were warm and his eyelids drooped seductively. His lips lifted slightly in one corner.

'All to ourselves.'

'Of course.'

* * * * *

If you enjoyed this story,
why not check out these other great reads
by Helen Dickson

Wedded for His Secret Child
Resisting Her Enemy Lord
A Viscount to Save Her Reputation
Enthralled by Her Enemy's Kiss
To Catch a Runaway Bride